Carl Weber's Kingpins:
Charlotte

Part 2

Carl Weber's Kingpins:
Charlotte

Part 2

Blake Karrington

www.urbanbooks.net

Urban Books, LLC
300 Farmingdale Road, N.Y.-Route 109
Farmingdale, NY 11735

Carl Weber's Kingpins: Charlotte; Part 2

ISBN 13: 978-1-64556-649-6
EBOOK ISBN: 978-1-64556-650-2

First Trade Paperback Printing August 2024
Printed in the United States of America

10 9 8 7 6 5 4 3 2 1

This is a work of fiction. Any references or similarities to actual events, real people, living or dead, or to real locales are intended to give the novel a sense of reality. Any similarity in other names, characters, places, and incidents is entirely coincidental.

Distributed by Kensington Publishing Corp.
Submit orders to:
Customer Service
400 Hahn Road
Westminster, MD 21157-4627
Phone: 1-800-733-3000
Fax: 1-800-659-2436

Carl Weber's Kingpins:
Charlotte

Part 2

Blake Karrington

Prologue

The Queen City, known to visitors and the rest of the world as Charlotte, North Carolina, was named after Queen Charlotte of Great Britain. The old bird would shit bricks if she knew that a black King was driving down the streets of the city named after her and feeling this good, King thought as he drove his new white Jaguar XJL through the center of his hometown. Usually, he would be checking his rearview and side mirrors for the fucking cops or some bitch-ass niggas who had beef with him or his crew. But tonight, he was riding on the high of it being Friday, and nothing but a good time was ahead. With the top down, the air caressed his freshly shaved face. He had just gotten the VIP late-night treatment from his barber, Don. It was after hours, and Don didn't do shit for anyone unless they made it worth his while, and dropping a C-note to ole boy had definitely made it worth it.

King checked his reflection in the mirror and smiled. His thin mustache was lined up perfectly, and his fade was cut very low. King's thick eyebrows highlighted his light brown eyes and long eyelashes. Genetics were a great thing. Even when he was young, people would always compliment him on his looks. He had his last growth spurt over the summer after he turned 13. He had shot up six inches, and his shoulders had broadened. He now stood six two, caramel skin, with a sculpted body that turned the heads of women and girls.

Tonight, he was feeling himself. Usually, he was on "ready, set, go," but for a brief moment, he was going to allow himself to chill.

He stopped at a red light, and a group of college girls walked by. They slowed down and seductively waved at King. He nodded at them and flashed his thousand-watt smile as they smiled back. The light turned green, and he hit the accelerator. Resting his right hand on his steering wheel, he allowed his left hand to hang over the door.

As he cruised, his mind drifted back to his teenage years, when he was just 16 years old.

King was in the driver's seat of his father's Mercedes. They were listening to Frankie Beverly & Maze's "Before I Let Go," which was his father's favorite song. King bobbed his head to the music while his father ran down some facts about the family business of hustling.

Reggie reached over and turned down the volume on the radio. "Listen, Ronnie," Reggie said, calling King by his first name, while looking out the passenger window. "Son, this life we in is like no other. These streets ain't got no love for no damn body. Games are for chumps, not for this business. This is some serious shit, and you can never underestimate a man's intentions when it comes to being on top. You feel me?" Reggie said.

King smiled as Reggie's voice and face began to fade into the side glass of the downtown building. His heart ached as the pain of losing his father at such a young age began to resurface. King took a deep breath. As he exhaled, his current world came back into view for him. As his mind cleared of his father, he pressed the volume button on the radio. Jay-Z's "Heart of the City (Ain't No Love)" pumped through the Bose speakers. *Damn, Dad kept it all the way real.*

He approached the top of the hill and dropped the car down into second gear. This was the perfect place to test out the power of his new toy. He looked at the clock. He had spent enough time bullshitting around. He was only about twenty minutes from his trap house. He needed to meet Strap, collect his money, and make sure those fools had everything bagged up. This was not the night to be running late. It was Friday, and the spot would have been booming all day with business. He didn't like to leave a lot of cash in the hood. It would tempt folks too much.

King took out his cell phone and called his boy, Strap, to make sure that everything was ready for him to pick up. The phone rang several times until the voicemail came on. King dialed Strap's number again. It rang twice this time, and then there was silence on the line for a brief second.

"Hey, yo, Strap. What up, fam?" King said as he turned down Milton Road. The silence on the line erupted into loud popping sounds.

"Strap? Hey, Strap, what the fuck is going on? Strap!" King yelled into his Bluetooth. He heard several more shots, and then the line clicked. "Strap, Strap!" King hurriedly pulled over in front of the old Circle K and jumped out. He was only a couple of blocks away from the dope house, and he needed to get his gun out of the trunk. One of his girls had reminded him that the biggest gang in the city, CMPD, were out heavy on the streets, and he needed to ride somewhat clean, especially on a Friday. King wasn't sure what he was about to walk into, but he knew he'd heard some heavy gunfire when he called Strap.

He placed the Glock in the back of his pants and jumped back in the car. Quickly, he popped it into gear and sped out toward the trap house. He killed his lights as he turned down Milton. The street was quiet as King slowly approached the house. He stopped two houses down from his destination, parked near some bushes that partially hid his car, and raised his top. The streetlights were shot out as usual. The power company had stopped replacing them.

King double-checked his clip and quietly made his way up to the trap house. As he approached, he could see someone slumped on the front steps. He ran over to the body and saw his man holding his stomach and moaning.

"Ah fuck, Strap! Shit," King said, kneeling beside him. "Damn, brah, where you hit?" King asked while Strap coughed and tried to pull himself up. "Nah, stay still. Who the fuck did this?" King said, holding his friend.

King heard a gurgling sound come from Strap as he took a deep breath. He placed his ear close to Strap's lips.

Strap took another breath. As he exhaled, he whispered a name to King. "Red." After uttering the name, his head dropped to the left.

"Shit! Strap, come on, man. You going to be a'ight. Stay with me, brah," King said. He shook his friend, but the light had left his eyes.

King wanted to scream, but he knew he needed to get inside to survey the full damage. He closed Strap's eyes and stood. The screen door screeched as he opened it and walked inside the house.

King kept his gun raised as he rounded the corner of the room. As he approached the kitchen, he could smell the blood and death in the air. Chris, Li'l T, and Monster lay on the old, cracked floor with bullets to the back of their heads and blood pooling around them.

"Fuck . . . Fuck!" King said as he scanned the room for any sign of his money or drugs. Nothing was there. All of it was gone.

In that moment, he didn't care about the money as his eyes fell on his fallen friends. He whispered a prayer to the God of his grandmother for their souls. The prayer of the thugs.

King stood and backed out of the kitchen. He left the house and paused as the body of one of his closest friends lay on the steps. He hated to just leave him there like that, but he knew there was nothing else he could do for his man except make sure the people who took his life lost theirs.

"Brah, I got you. Them niggas gonna pay for this shit!" King said before jumping down the steps.

He sprinted back to the bushes and jumped in his car, made a U-turn, and headed back up Milton. As he drove down the street, he checked his rearview for any potential assailants or witnesses who may have been lurking. He was sure that the cops were probably only minutes away, and as he turned onto Plaza Road, he heard the sirens. Shifting the gears as he made his way to Harris Boulevard, he could feel his blood boil as he thought about Strap and his other homeboys. His heartbeat rang in his ears. He needed to get to somewhere quick so he could process everything, and he needed someone he could trust. His family was what he needed.

King headed toward his mother and stepfather's house. There, he would find sanctuary to piece together his thoughts and find a solution as to what he should do next. Carlton, King's stepfather, had stepped up when his biological father passed away from a heart attack. King was 18 when his father passed, and Carlton was right there for him and his mother. Carlton was his father's best friend, and in many ways, he was just like King's daddy. They both were old-school street dudes who knew the game and played it well. King had never seen either of them without a custom suit, tie, and a starched shirt. King and Carlton were as close as two people who shared the same DNA.

As he pulled up to his parents' home, he checked the time. It was late, and King had a second thought about going inside. He didn't want to wake them up, but he knew that Carlton would be upset if he was not told about the robbery. Using his key, he let himself into the quiet house. He could tell that his mother had decorated yet again. The living room that once had a country theme now had earth-tone colors and African art on the walls, with little elephants, lions, and monkey figurines placed around the room. Hearing the TV, King shook his head and made his way downstairs to the basement.

Carlton was sitting in his favorite recliner watching an episode of *Law & Order*. "Hey, son!" Carlton said, putting the TV on mute.

King gave him a weak smile as he sat down. He could see the butt of Carlton's Smith & Wesson on the side of the chair, and he was sure there was more firepower all around that room. The smile was short, and the anxiety of the evening returned.

Carlton took a sip of his Hennessy and slid to the end of the chair. "What's going on, son? Talk to me."

King looked up at him and dropped his head back down. "They dead, all of them. Dead," King stated, fighting back tears. He ran his hands over his face and lay back on the couch. As soon as he closed his eyes, he felt sick to his stomach when Strap's lifeless stare entered his mind again.

"Who dead?" Carlton said and stood up.

"All my boys at the trap house, Strap, Li'l T, Chris, and Monster. They murked all of them and took the money and dope. Shit, Strap died in my damn arms. I know my nigga got a couple of shots off for sure. Before he died, he told me this nigga named Red did it."

Carlton could see the hurt in King's eyes and the fury. He sighed and sat back down in his recliner, shaking his head as he sipped his Hen.

King stood and walked over to the bar. He grabbed a glass and poured himself a drink. After swirling it around for a moment, he sipped it. Both men were quiet for what seemed like forever.

"I'm going to get them niggas, though, and I'm going to start with Red's ass. They going to get dealt with real soon," King screamed.

"Son," Carlton responded while lighting one of his cigars, "in our business, murder brings attention we don't want or need. Murder results in bodies, and bodies result in investigation by the cops. I know you ready to wage war, but we gotta let this cool for a minute. You gotta be smart about your moves, and check your damn emotions. Keep it in your mind, but don't act too soon. I know you want vengeance right now, but let's just wait," Carlton said, blowing circles of smoke in the air.

King shook his head and allowed the Hennessy to flow down his throat as he listened to his stepfather. "Yeah, let them rest easy for now. But believe me, I am going to have Red and his crew crying like little bitches when I'm done with them."

"Such language," a soft voice said from the stairs.

King managed to flash a smile at the beautiful woman who emerged from the stairwell. His mother wore a long silk robe with the belt tied tightly around her small waist, which accentuated her hips. The gold and diamond cross that she wore around her neck touched the heart-shaped tattoo she had on her chest with the name Reggie, King's father, inside of it. Yolanda, or Yogi, as everyone called her, was in her late forties, but she had the body of a 19-year-old. Her caramel skin was near perfect. She had large brown eyes, full lips, high hips, and her long, relaxed hair flowed down her back. Yolanda was a natural beauty and a true Southern lady. She was soft-spoken, elegant, and graceful. She could enter a room without saying a word, and heads would turn. At least that was the Yolanda side of her. The Yogi side was the complete opposite. She was street educated and would always let you know just what she felt and was ready to whoop some ass if anyone disagreed with what she was saying. King was her only child, and she had vowed to make sure he had everything he could ever want, and she would do anything to make that happen.

Yogi smiled at them both and stretched her arms out to King.

Carlton stood and walked to the bar. He grabbed a glass and poured Yogi a drink.

"Hey, baby, I thought I heard someone come in. It's good to see you," Yogi said, hugging her son tightly.

King felt the anger and despair that had consumed him moments ago lift as his mother hugged him. Carlton touched her back and handed her the glass.

Yogi flashed a smile at him and kissed his cheek. "Well, I will let you men get back to business," Yogi said, making her way toward the stairs. "Oh, and Sunday dinner will be served at four. I don't care how late you are out tonight, you better not be late."

King laughed and nodded. His mother cut her eyes at him playfully and blew him a kiss.

"Night, Ma," King said as she walked back up the stairs.

Chapter One

King awoke from a long nap while sitting in the terminal waiting for his flight to board. That dream had taken him through a brief part of his life that had placed him on the path to this moment. His back pressed against the hard plastic bench, his fingers now tapping on the smooth surface of his phone screen. The seat cushion beneath him shifted as he adjusted his weight, and the cool metal of his watch brushed against his wrist with each movement.

His meeting had gone well, and he was pleased with how things were looking for Sloan's career.

There was no money like dope money, but there was also something about knowing that he could make a grip of money the legal way. He didn't have to worry that the Feds would come, he didn't have to worry about cases being built, or indictments, and the music business was very lucrative. If he was going to step away from the drug game and toward something legit, the music business was a good choice. Still, even though the meeting went well, King was still uneasy. Since Tiana's death, he couldn't sleep. His heart ached for his friend, and the cruel reminder of what came with the game made him want to exit that much faster. He lived one hell of a life, and he had enough memories to last a lifetime. King was ready to bow out gracefully, but there were some things he had to do first.

He knew that Kareem wouldn't be able to rest until the people responsible for Tiana's death were dealt with. Not even that would bring her back, but it would be a start. King was haunted by thoughts of Kordell, Keana, and KJ growing up without their mother. All Tiana wanted was for Kareem to leave the game because she feared him dying or going to jail, and she was the one who ended up losing her life. The shit wasn't fair. It wasn't fair at all, and King was becoming sick and tired of the never-ending battles that came with being who he was. He was ready to wave that white flag.

His cell phone rang, interrupting his thoughts. With weary eyes, he glanced at the screen and saw that Sloan was calling. Things were picking up for her quite fast, and she was in Atlanta meeting with a very famous producer who requested she sing on one of his tracks. That was an absolute honor, and King didn't waste any time booking her the flight.

"What's good?" he asked, relieved that she was able to distract him from the feeling of sadness that had suddenly consumed him.

"That's what I'm trying to find out. How did the meeting go?"

"It went quite well actually. I will be boarding the plane in about two minutes, and there is no way that I can run down everything that was covered in the meeting. Just know that people are fucking with you, and there are some very good deals being placed on the table. You don't even have an album out yet, and I got an email earlier about a possible endorsement," King stated with pride. Being a rookie in the business had some people trying to come at him like he didn't know what he was doing. He even had a label suggest that he give them Sloan. It felt good knowing that he was helping her to get to the level that she desired without him having much experience in the business. King was going to prove everyone who doubted him wrong. Sloan was going to be the next Rihanna or Beyoncé, and he was willing to bet the bank on that. The squeal that she let out made him aware that she was pleased also.

"That's awesome. Thank you so much for all you've done for me, my love. I will be wrapping up here around the time your plane lands, and then I'll be heading back to Charlotte tonight. If I'm not too tired, maybe we can discuss things over dinner."

"That sounds like a plan, babe."

King smiled as he ended the call. An announcement was made that first class could start boarding the plane, and he stood up. Soon, instead of dope deals and getting revenge on enemies, he'd just be a businessman catching flights and closing deals, and he was looking forward to it.

Panama sat on the porch of the old farmhouse. The home was nestled in the middle of over one hundred acres of land that his family had owned, going well back to the early 1900s. The cows grazed on the high grass, as the chickens were clucking in their pen. It took Panama a minute to get his nasals used to the smell of chicken shit and rotten meat. His grandfather still herded cattle, raised hogs, and talked shit like he had always done for the last eighty-five years. Although he had moved from the old farmhouse years ago, and built himself a little ranch-style home away from the smell of the cows and other animals, Panama had told his grandfather that he should leave the old house standing since it was a part of their family's history. He promised that he would fix it up for him, and they could use it as a guest house during holiday visits from the rest of the family.

He had intentions of, eventually, fixing the home up. For right now he would be using it for the business at hand. Panama had made one upgrade, soundproof rooms, and tonight he would have his first guests since his remodel. Checking his watch, he leaned back in the old wooden rocking chair. He placed his earbuds in his ears and allowed J. Cole's music to massage his mind. His phone chirped, momentarily interrupting his vibe, and he checked the message and stretched. Grabbing the large black leather bag, he headed downstairs toward the cellar. Walking over to the table, he gazed down at the hammers, scalpels, and small-caliber handguns spread out like an arsenal buffet. It was early morning, and the sun was just starting to shine. Panama loved this time of day on the farm, as this part of the land had no trees to stop the sun's rays from beaming down.

Cool-man and the crew should be pulling up at any time with their guests, and Kareem was sitting on the couch staring off into space. Since the murder of his one true love, Tiana, his entire personality had changed. He became quiet and withdrawn. Panama actually preferred this version of him better, as at least now he was focused instead of always joking around. Losing his girl was a high price to pay, but at least now he truly understood that this street life wasn't a fucking game. In their business, one mistake could cost you and your loved ones everything.

"How much longer they gon' be, Panama?" Shine asked as he cleaned his nails with a knife.

"They on their way, nigga. Just sit tight, and grab ya'self a cold one out the frig, my G," Panama said, touching the hammer.

"Reem, you sho' these the niggas who know what happened to ya girl?"

Kareem shook his head. His eyes had not left the window. King was in New York handling some business for Sloan, he knew he would be back later that evening, but Kareem had no intention of waiting on him. He would handle these suckas in his own way. He knew Panama could make anyone talk, as the nigga's mind was something that nightmares were created from. Kareem had always figured it was due to his military training, but meeting his grandfather, and listening to his tales of old gangster days, he knew that Panama had inherited that shit. Just listening to the old man speak last night seemed to make the temperature drop. The backwoods country had really produced some cold-ass niggas.

The sound of tires hitting the gravel got everyone's attention. They all stood and started heading for the door, just as two large black vans pulled in front of the home, followed by a trail of dust. Kareem froze. Trip touched his shoulder and gently pushed him back.

"Let Pan set thangs up first, then you can get at them. A'ight?"

Kareem shook his head. He didn't realize that he was grinding his teeth until Trip looked at him like he had lost his mind. "You need to relax, bro, we got this."

Panama recognized the ink on the arm of one of the men. It was from a unit that he was familiar with from the first Gulf War. No wonder it had taken eight of his boys to subdue this motherfucker. One of them had a broken collarbone and another one a broken arm. Kareem walked down the stairs. As he placed his foot on the last step, Panama raised the Magnum as the three men sat with hoods over their heads, and two could be heard whimpering, but the third one sat still. Panama had the gun to the back of the man's head. He squeezed the trigger, firing into the back of the third man's head.

Panama took two steps closer and fired again. The two men began struggling against their restraints, and one of them urinated, and the liquid splashed against the plastic that covered the floor beneath their chairs. Kareem walked over past Panama, and he reached down and pulled the black bag off the head of the man. Pieces of his skull and brain hit the floor. Kareem stepped back, trying to make sure nothing had gotten on his shoes.

"Fuck! What the hell? We need to get some answers from them first."

"That one was never going to tell us anything."

"How you know that?" Kareem asked, looking for something to wipe the blood from his hand.

"It will probably be best that you leave, Kareem, and I will let you know what I find out."

"I ain't going no fucking where," Kareem said, taking a seat on the small stool by the window. The window had been covered with a black garbage bag, making the basement dark. There was only one light that hung from the ceiling, providing the only brightness in the huge basement.

Panama exhaled and jerked the hood from the other two men's heads.

"Gentlemen, welcome to the Farms. You will be guests here for a few days, and it is up to you as to how comfortable your stay will be while you're here," Panama said, smiling at the two terrified men.

"Nigga, you have lost your mind. Do you know who the fuck we are? You don't fuck with our crew! You gonna burn for this shit!" the man on the left yelled as he struggled with his restraints.

Kareem stood, and he looked at the man. He had a long scar on the left side of his face that went from below his eye to the corner of his mouth.

Panama laughed and began removing the man's shoes and socks. He walked over to a table and removed five shoestrings that had been soaking in some type of liquid. He tied the string to each of the toes on the man's left foot.

"Ask your questions," Panama said, stepping back and looking at Kareem.

"Who told you to put the bomb in the truck?" Kareem asked.

"What? I don't know nothing about no fucking bomb!"

Panama took out a match and lit the end of the shoe-string. Stepping on the man's foot as the string began to burn, the fire starting to circle his toe, Panama slid a piece of metal between the big toe and second toe. The man screamed out in pain from the hot metal.

Shine looked up from his phone as the smell of burning flesh began to fill the room. He reached over and turned on the exhaust fan and went back to playing *Candy Crush* on his phone.

Sloan stared at herself in the mirror, and she rinsed her mouth out with water and wiped her face with a wet paper towel. Her head was pounding, and her lower abdomen cramped. She cursed herself for gorging on those crab legs. They were tasty last night, and she was paying for it, but she needed to get this track laid down today. She was sure the engineer was grateful to her for not vomiting the seafood all over his studio equipment.

"Sloan, you okay?" Mona asked as she knocked on the bathroom door.

"Yeah, just give me a few minutes, and I will be right out," Sloan responded as she grabbed a dry paper towel and wiped her mouth. She smoothed back her hair and checked her clothes. She opened the door. Mona stood by the entrance and jumped when Sloan opened it.

"Hey, you okay?" Mona said, rubbing Sloan's back. "Shit, you are pale as fuck."

"Yeah, I think the crab legs are crawling back up," Sloan said, holding her stomach.

"Damn, you just gave me a visual that makes me not want to eat them shits for a while!" Mona said, laughing. "You want me to tell Boo that you need to cancel?"

"Girl, no, we need to get this done. I'm going to be fine. Can you find me some seltzer water?" Sloan asked as she walked back into the recording room. Mona nodded and disappeared down the hall.

"You a'ight, baby girl?" Boo asked.

"Yeah, I'm okay. Let's get this done."

Boo nodded, and Sloan placed back on the headset as Boo cued up the track for the song. She hummed, closing her eyes. Sloan followed the notes that flowed through the headset.

I bet you don't know
How to love anymore
That is why you're walking toward that door
Loving me and loving you
Is just too much work for us to do

Sloan loved the way the saxophone sounded on the track. She wanted this song to be sexy and sad. It was what women wanted and needed. Everybody somewhere was breaking up, and music was better than therapy when you needed to get over a broken heart. Sloan cheered when Boo gave her the thumbs-up.

"Gold like always, baby girl," he said, clapping.

"Thanks, Boo. Whew, I'm tired, but I'm glad I was able to push through," Sloan stated with relief. She knew this dream of hers wouldn't come easy. She had just managed to stay in a studio for hours perfecting a song while it felt like there was a war going on in her belly. All she wanted was a bed, but she had created an entire song all while feeling like shit. Sloan was quite proud of herself. Mona handed her a ginger ale.

"We didn't have any seltzer water. I will make sure they have some next time."

"I hope this will pass. My grandmother just always gave me seltzer water when my stomach was upset. The ginger ale should be just as good. I think I am going to head to the hotel and lay it down. I have two hours before my flight, and I'm right by the airport. It was such a pleasure working with you, Boo." Sloan grabbed her black Michael Kors tassel bag, and gave Mona a hug before walking out the door. Moose followed her down the long hallway. She still had a difficult time adjusting to having security, but King had insisted that she have it when he wasn't around. Moose opened the passenger door to the SUV, and Sloan winced as a sharp pain hit her lower stomach again.

"You okay?" he asked, concerned.

"Yeah, I'm okay. I think that the crab legs are having their revenge on me," Sloan said, holding her belly. "I just need to get to the hotel and take some medicine. I pray it's not food poisoning," she groaned while Moose nodded and closed the door.

Several hours had passed, and they knew no more than they did when they started. Kareem punched the wall and walked up the stairs. Either these niggas liked being tortured or they were not high enough up in the organization to know anything of use. Shine and Trip dragged the men outside as the sun was going down, lighting the sky up with an orange glow. The men moaned in pain from the hours of torture that Panama and Kareem had put them through.

Trip and Shine dropped them to the ground under a tall oak tree. Shine was the youngest, and he wanted to make a little money watching the trap and maybe beating a nigga down every once in a while. This shit was on another level. The men had been beaten so badly they didn't even look human anymore. He didn't have the stomach for this type of shit.

Kareem picked up a tire and slid it over the heavy-set dude's head, and liquid sloshed from inside the tire. Shine and Trip looked at each other as Kareem did the same to the second man.

Kareem took out the grill lighter he had picked up while in the basement. Closing his eyes, he saw the truck with flames jumping out of it. He could hear Tiana crying out to him, as she struggled to get out of the burning vehicle. The only woman he'd ever loved in that way had been charred, cooked alive. Opening his eyes, before tears could fill them, he looked at the badly beaten men. Deep down inside he knew that they didn't know anything, but he needed to make someone pay for his pain. Even if these two didn't have any information he could use, they were as close as he could get to the people who did at the moment. Kareem glared at them.

Trip and Shine stood back watching.

"You know, on her last birthday, I gave my baby a necklace, and now I'ma give yo' asses one." The first man looked up at him with pleading eyes hoping for some form of mercy, but there was none. Kareem placed the lighter to the tire, and immediately the fire began to blaze. The man yelled and began to struggle. Kareem walked over to the other man, who was semiconscious, and lit the second tire. The heat licking at his skin woke him.

Trip and Shine could not move. Both stood and watched in horror. As the bodies of the two men began to wither from the heat of the flames, Shine turned his head and started vomiting in the high grass, and the men's screams echoed through the air. Shine wanted to run to the car, and he looked at Kareem, who seemed to be mesmerized by the men's pain and torture. Trip took out his phone and dialed Panama.

"Yeah," Panama said as he cut the sandwich in half for his grandfather and placed it on the table. "Y'all done?"

"Yeah, your boy just necklaced these niggas. Pan, he done lost his fucking mind. I ain't seen no shit like this since we were—"

"What you mean necklaced?" Panama said as he placed the glass of tea on the table for his grandfather. He nearly dropped the phone after hearing that word. The only time he heard it was when he was on tour in Africa fifteen years ago. He had seen a lot of shit, and he had tried to forget most of it. The shit he saw in Africa still visited him on the nights when he didn't take something to sleep.

"Man, you need to get out here. Trip done spit up his lunch, and I ain't far behind him."

Panama could hear the men screaming, and his blood chilled in his veins as he hung up the phone.

"Pops, I got to handle something at the old house. You all right?"

"Yeah, yeah, I'm fine, just hand me the remote control. I like that moonshining show. I'm two episodes behind, and they building a kettle still. Making me want to get back in the business."

"Yeah, we'll talk about that when I get back." Panama laughed and closed the door, and he walked out onto the porch. The sun was setting, and that meant that Panama wouldn't be able to see much of anything on the golf cart when it got dark. The lights were not that bright, and since it wasn't used for getting around at night, he wasn't even sure if they even worked.

As he made his way through the path to the old farm house, he could smell the sickening odor of flesh burning. He turned left at the path, and he drove toward the smoke. Trip and Shine were standing back, and Kareem seemed to be in a trance as he watched the last flicker of life in the men. Panama pulled his Magnum from the waist of his pants, and with two clean shots the little life left in them was gone, putting them both out of their misery. Kareem didn't move. Trip and Shine walked over to Panama.

"That is some fucked-up shit. Pan, this nigga is gone, man. His head is gone. I ain't ever seen no shit like that!" Trip repeated.

Panama shook his head. Kareem stood motionless, his eyes locked on the body of the burning men.

"Man, I can't clean this shit up. Pan, you gonna need to get somebody else for this shit," Trip uttered.

"Y'all can head back to the city, and don't mention this shit to nobody."

The men nodded.

"Hey, I mean it. Don't talk about this shit to no one," Panama added, and looking back at Kareem, he exhaled. He needed to get this mess cleaned up before the sun came up and the horror of what happened was out in the open. No one ever came around, but still. This wasn't anything that he wanted to risk the wrong person seeing.

Chapter Two

Yogi fastened the diaper on Caleb as the baby cooed and blew spit bubbles.

"Look at you, look at you. That was a stinky one," Yogi said, waving her hand in front of her face. Caleb laughed, and Yogi placed the diaper in the trash can, washed her hands, and grabbed the diaper bag. She picked Caleb up and closed the changing table. He was a beautiful baby, and he had Yogi wrapped around his little finger. His large brown eyes and curly hair made people mistake him for a girl at times. She placed him in the stroller, and he began to fuss as she searched the diaper bag for his pacifier. The bathroom door opened, and a young woman walked in, and she smiled at Yogi and looked at Caleb.

"He is adorable! What a doll," the young woman said, tickling Caleb's tummy. "Is Mama taking you out for some sun and ice cream? Is she?"

Yogi laughed. "He's my godson. I am way too old to be having babies. My baby is twenty-seven years old."

"What? You don't look like you are old enough to even have a teenager! Girl, what is your secret?"

Yogi laughed. "You are kind. I don't have a secret. Just loving life, I guess," Yogi spoke, looking at Caleb.

"Well, put it in a bottle and sell me some," the woman responded, walking into the stall.

"You have a good day," Yogi uttered while opening the door and pushing Caleb's stroller out.

Carlton sat on the park bench, and he waved to Yogi as she walked toward him. The last few months had been bearable with him. Yogi wished she could love Carlton the way she had before, but his infidelities made that difficult. He made an effort to win her back and to build her confidence in his promise to be faithful to her. Still, when she looked at him, the little shudder she used to feel when she looked at him was gone. She felt more loyalty than passion or love for Carlton now.

"So the next one is yours. Whew, this boy lets them go like a grown man. He took my breath away!"

"He gotcha, huh? Well, give him to me. I'll take him on the swing," Carlton said, taking the diaper bag from Yogi and placing it under the stroller. He picked up Caleb. With drool pooled under his little chin, his little face frowned as he passed gas and cooed.

"Boy, what have you been eating?" Carlton said, laughing, Yogi wiped Caleb's chin and placed his little Charlotte Hornets baseball cap on his head. Carlton walked over to the swing set, holding Caleb in his right arm.

Yogi watched Carlton swing with him, and a slight shudder returned to her stomach. She loved taking care of Caleb. It took her back to when King was a baby. She sighed thinking of how she wished she could turn back time and protect him from the world. He was no longer the little baby she could put in his playpen and shield. He was a grown man out in the world. At the moment, it felt like the world was coming for her baby hard and fast.

Chapter Three

King watched Chin's boys put three large duffel bags in the back of the Cadillac truck. They took over Woo's trap houses over the last three months. The streets were silent about Woo's disappearance and how Chin's boys had set up the operation. The passenger door opened, and Panama sat down beside him.

"They moving some heavy shit. Looks like that China White," Panama spoke as they watched the men reup the workers and then drive off, and all the dope boys began serving the fiends new goods.

"Fuck them niggas though. We can handle them. What I need to talk to you about is Kareem," Panama said, looking in the rearview mirror. "This thing with his girl has really messed with that nigga's head, and he doing some dangerous shit."

King nodded in agreement. Kareem's grief was something that he didn't seem to have the ability to work through. Yogi advised him to give Kareem time. Losing the one you love the way that he did was going to take a while for him to get over. Lately he became withdrawn and angry all the time. The nigga made it his mission to find out who was responsible for taking Tiana away from him and the kids. Kareem still couldn't shake back from the fear of what would have happened if the kids had been in the truck with Tiana. Somebody had to pay for this shit and soon.

"We had two guys we thought was connected to the bombing. I worked them over pretty good, but they didn't know shit. You know I like to do my shit clean. I do a job with discretion and don't move on emotion."

"So what happened?"

"Kareem necklaced those dudes. I ain't seen that shit since Africa. That shit right there is one of the worst things you can do to a nigga."

"You mean that shit with the tires?"

"Yeah. You gotta do something with him, King. He is not in his right mind right now. You know I ain't ever liked the way he handled business before. I know that's your boy, but he was too much of a jokester for me. Now he's doing this shit without thinking of how that could have gone wrong. I know we were out in the boonies, but I don't do shit to cause any attention."

King looked down at his watch and back over at Panama. "Yeah, this life right here, it ain't meant to be long term. Shit, like what happened to Tiana is the reason we need to get out as soon as we can, playboy. You know what my pop's passion was? His passion was music. Not too many people know that, but he actually had a decent voice, and he played the sax, man."

"What?" Panama said, turning to King, laughing. King's father was a gangster's gangster and was only known for hustling and taking anyone out who got in his way.

"Yeah, man, he did. My mother didn't know until after I was born that he sang and played. She went to the store and came back one day to hear him singing to me in my crib. She said I was laughing and trying to sing along with him. I guess that's where I get my love of music. Also, I'm tired of this shit, bruh. I feel like an old man in these streets. The only reason I'm still keeping this hustle going is because I got loyal people with families to feed. They don't know anything else."

Panama nodded as he watched two more niggas pull up to the trap house. He recognized one of them as Chin, but the taller one was new. Chin stopped to check his reflection in the mirror and then began walking up the driveway of the house.

"Word on the street is this nigga Chin lost a big load to some Jamaican dudes, and his supplier wanted his money or his dick on a platter from what I understand," Panama spoke while pointing in Chin's direction.

"Yeah, well, it looks like he done made his money back now, and Texas's ass is more than happy to try to serve my side of the city to these motherfuckers. Dobbs say that our sales are down, two of the houses got hit last week, and he took a big hit. Charlotte ain't big enough for all this traffic, and all this shit will bring attention if it ain't already done it. The fucking Feds will come head-first into this shit. What's them dudes' names from Lancaster?" King asked.

"Oh, you mean them little young niggas who came up here and took over Bowling Road?"

"Yeah, them. We need to take that shit from them. They ain't organized, and from what I hear they inexperienced and scary. I got Raleigh, Greensboro, and working on Wilmington to get on line. We had to chill out in Fayetteville for a minute because some shit got too hot last month, and that took a big chunk outta our bottom line. I need for the boys to go up to the store and bring back what we got left up there. I ain't going to lose hold on my city. Even if I need to get out on the front line of this shit, this is still my city until I let it go."

Texas put the clip into the AK and squeezed the trigger. Feeling the vibrations of the automatic weapon in his hands calmed his nerves. His little cousin, Bobo, had been missing for a few days along with two of his other men. Bobo's mama called him every day asking about him and the money that he was supposed to send to her and his sister. Texas had wired them a stack, and he had Mack take them three more stacks on his way down to Atlanta. At first he thought that Bobo had been lying up with some ass, but when he didn't answer any of his calls or texts, Texas knew something was up. He had brought the little nigga up from Atlanta to learn the game and to feed his family. He had hardly left Texas's side since coming to NC, and now he was ghost.

Texas put the gun down on the concrete slab and checked his phone. He had no missed calls or messages from Jytia, as a matter of fact, she had little communication with him over the last few days. She had officially moved into Red's old place. She said her people were getting tired of her not coming home and had grilled her too much about her business. She had been managing some of Red's shit, and she was a fucking quick study. She had been moving bricks from Atlanta to New York and making a significant profit. New York was a different beast, but from what his boy Wally told him, Jytia had made some smart moves with purchasing a property and moving her shit without issue from cops or other niggas.

His phone buzzed, and Chin's number popped up on the screen. Texas sighed. Chin was a careless dude, and careless dudes got your ass a bullet or a prison number. He let voicemail answer Chin, and he picked up the assault weapon and began firing at the target. After emptying three clips, Texas grabbed the gun and walked back to his truck. He placed the gun under the seat in a lockbox and pulled out of the field. He tuned the radio to WPEG and bobbed his head to Drake. He pulled into the parking lot of Pat's convenience store. Some hood rats turned around when they saw the black F-150 pull up. Texas smiled at one who wore black yoga pants with a short black shirt. The sun hit her ass, showing that she had no panties on. He tried to guess her age, but with these little hot-ass girls nowadays, it was hard to tell without talking to them.

"I like yo' truck," the girl said, smiling.

Texas winked his eye as he pushed the door. Pat's had the best wings and potato wedges in West Charlotte.

"Texas, hey, baby, I ain't seen you in a while. Had me a little worried," the older black woman said as she wrote a price on the brown bag and handed it to another customer.

"Hey, Ms. Pat. Nah, I'm still above ground for now. How your family doing?"

"They all right, baby. What you want today? I got some fresh fried chicken livers."

"Whoo, yeah, give me some of them, ten wings, and five wedges."

Pat laughed and began placing the wings in the white bag. "Oh Lord, here come this thang," Ms Pat said, cutting her eyes toward the door.

"Hey, Texas!" Peaches bellowed. "I thought that was your truck the damn buzzards were circling outside. Damn, you looking sexy as fuck."

"Hey, Peaches, what's good with you?" Texas said, taking his phone out, hoping she would keep her ass moving.

"Ain't shit going on. I'm working when I should be up in my man's house being taken care of like he would have wanted," Peaches said, leaning against the counter. "But that little bitch up in my shit like she a fucking queen or something. I hear you hitting that shit, too. Damn, she community property now, huh? What she got in her twat that she got you like she had King?"

"Here you go. Come on over so I can ring ya up," Ms. Pat said, looking at Texas.

Texas smiled and walked over to the register. He looked out the door to see if little mama with the fat ass was still outside. The girl was leaning against a white Honda, talking to some other girls and laughing.

"A'ight, it is ten dollars and seventy-five cents," Ms. Pat said. "You don't want anything to drink? I just made some sweet tea."

"Ms. Pat, you know I need some of your sweet tea."

"So you gonna let me hold something? It's been hard keeping my bills up with Red gone. Shit, bitch 'bout to put in an application and work a regular job to make ends meet," Peaches said, rubbing Texas's back. Peaches was still fine as hell, but when she opened her mouth, the physical melted into a pile of shit.

Texas reached in his back pocket and pulled out five crisp $100 bills. He placed them in Peaches' hand, he handed Ms. Pat a twenty, and he began to walk out the door. He clicked the alarm on the truck and placed his food on the floor of the passenger side. The girl smiled at him as he approached the group.

"Good afternoon, ladies. How is everyone?"

The girls laughed and said, "Fine," in unison.

"I'm Texas. What's your name?" Texas scanned her. Now that he was closer, he could tell she was well over 18. Her large brown eyes stared straight through his chest as she was looking him up and down. Her long black bone-straight hair flowed down her back, and her toenails were painted a bright green color matching the nails on her hands. She was a pretty girl with a china doll face and an intriguing smile.

"Hi, Texas, I'm Donna," she whispered, extending her hand.

"Texas! Texas!" Peaches screeched as she walked up. "I know you ain't treating me like these cheap-ass tricks out here. What is this shit?" Peaches said, flinging the money in Texas's face. "You know this some bullshit. I can't even wipe my ass with this. Red must be turning over in his grave knowing y'all ain't doing what you need to be doing! I am far above this pocket change." Peaches stepped between Texas and Donna, and she put her finger in the middle of his forehead and pushed him back. "Nigga, do you hear me?"

"Umm, excuse me. We were talking," Donna said, taking a step away from the door of the Honda. Peaches turned around to see Donna standing wide-legged with her hands on her hips.

"Bitch, mind your business, and go chase another dick. Right now, I have business to discuss. Get in your fucking Honda and ride out while you can." Peaches turned back around to Tex. "Like I was saying, what is this shit? That ain't even gonna cover my damn hair and shit."

"From the looks of it, it will more than cover the hair, nails, and damn outfit with change to spare," Donna said, high-fiving her girlfriends.

Tex snickered but could see Peaches' temper begin to boil.

She turned around and with one swift swing swung at Donna, who moved out of the way just in time for Peaches to crack her fist on the window of the car. Peaches screamed as the bones in her hand cracked. Fueled by adrenaline, she swung at Donna again with her left hand.

Texas knew he should grab her, but li'l mama seemed to have the situation under control.

"You little low-rent hood-rat bitch!" Peaches said, lunging for Donna, who again moved out of Peaches' grasp.

"Look, take that money and take your ass back to the pole. You really don't want none of me. I'm being nice right now," Donna said, looking at Texas. Peaches tried to flex her right hand.

"You think he wants to talk to some little convenience store thot like you, ho? Shit, he just wants to use that mouth as a toilet, then be on his way, bitch!" Peaches said as she spat on Donna's toe. The girls with Donna stepped back. Donna landed a right hook on the side of Peaches' face and then a left upper cut. Texas's mouth fell open as Donna laid in punches like fucking Mayweather on Peaches, who couldn't get her bearing together quick enough to avoid the punches. Two of Peaches' friends from the club appeared, and Donna's friend's blocked them from getting into the fight. Donna grabbed Peaches by the back of her head.

"Let me up!"

Texas watched, not believing he was seeing Peaches submit to anyone. This li'l chick was a beast! Donna yanked Peaches' head back.

"Donna, that's enough now," Ms. Pat said from the door of the store. "Send her on."

She looked at Ms. Pat and sighed. Donna let go of Peaches' head and collected the money that Texas had given her from the ground. She shoved the money at Peaches. "Get your ugly ass out of here before I fuck your ass up, skank!" Donna's friends let Peaches' friends through, and they helped her to her feet and walked to the blue SUV by the gas tank.

Texas watched as they peeled out of the parking lot, barely missing hitting a car. Donna motioned to the girls to get in the car.

"I don't do drama. I got to go."

"Hey, wait. I'm sorry about that. Peaches can be a little emotional at times."

"Looks like you got her more than emotional! I didn't picture you dating no old-ass stripper," Donna said, grabbing her purse and taking out a wipe. She wiped her foot off and checked her reflection in the mirror. "Shit, I chipped a damn nail, and now I need to go soak my damn feet in bleach. Your baby mama is something."

Texas looked at Donna, and he couldn't hold in his laughter as he looked at the disgusted expression on her face.

"Nah, nah, baby girl, you got that all wrong. First, a nigga ain't got no kids, and second, I'll cut my dick off before I get that chick pregnant. Nah, that is a partner of mine's ex."

"A partner's? Boy, whatever. I got to go," Donna said, opening the door to her car.

"Hold up, hold up. Give a nigga a few minutes, please," Texas said, smiling at Donna.

Donna closed the door and leaned back on the car.

"On the real, my partner was murdered a few weeks back, and Peaches was his girl. He took care of her, and now that he is gone, she feels like I should be keeping her up. Look, she ain't no issue. She's just crazy."

Donna sighed. Her light brown eyes sparkled as she looked up at Texas.

"You can ask Ms. Pat. I'm good people."

"Is that right? You just have psycho strippers hanging around you on a regular?"

Texas laughed, and although Donna wanted to be angry, she couldn't resist his smile.

"I tell you what, since you messed up your cute feet and your nails, go have them done on me. Do you know Nichelle's Nails?"

"Yeah, down on the Tuck?"

"Go take your girls, and go in there and get yourself treated to whatever you want, and tell her to bill Texas. Then if you forgive me, hit me up on my cell," Texas spoke, handing her his card. Donna took the card and got in her car. Texas winked at her and walked to his truck.

"Nichelle's Nails. That spot is crazy expensive, girl!" Latia said, pounding Meeka.

"That nigga mad sexy, too, umph," Meeka said, licking her lips. "What is up with that bitch?"

"Who the fuck cares? Bet she ain't gon' step to nobody like that again. She probably really need that money now that Donna fucked up her face!" Latia said, laughing.

Donna watched as Texas drove out of the parking lot. Yes, Texas looked delicious, and she couldn't wait to find out how he tasted.

Chapter Four

Sloan lay on the couch, watching one of her favorite Investigation Discovery shows, *Web of Lies*. Her stomach finally stopped doing somersaults, and her appetite returned. She picked up her phone and called King.

"Hey, bae," King answered.

"Hey, how are you, my love?" Sloan asked, pressing the mute button on the remote.

"I'm good, sitting here talking to big Pan. What's up?"

"I'm hungry. Can we go get something to eat?"

King laughed. Sloan was always hungry but never seemed to put on any weight.

"Uh, yeah, you wanna meet?"

"I'd rather you swing by and pick me up. I'm at home," Sloan said, stretching.

"Yeah, okay, babe. Give me about forty-five minutes?"

"Okay, love you." The line clicked.

King looked at the screen and then placed the phone back in the console.

"Everything all right?" Panama asked without looking at King. He watched the cars pull up to the trap house that Chin had gone into. So far at least nine other niggas had gone inside since Chin had arrived.

"Yeah, yeah, I guess," King said. "What are these fools doing? Having a meeting at a trap house? Who the fuck does that shit?"

"I don't know, but we ain't the only ones watching their asses," Panama said, nodding to the black Chevrolet

Impala sitting on the opposite side of the street. They had been there since the cars started coming up.

"Huh," King said as he started his car. "Where you park?"

"About three blocks over. I can walk back. Let me know what you're gonna do about your boy. He gotta be dealt with and dealt with soon. Give his ass something to concentrate on." Panama closed the door and pulled the hood up over his head.

King watched as he walked around the corner and disappeared down the street. King turned onto Kalley Street and looked back in his rearview at the Chevrolet. The little Camry he was in didn't draw unwanted attention and blended in with most neighborhoods. He would stop off at the warehouse to get his Benz and then pick up Sloan.

Imani smiled as Derrick opened the passenger car door, and she took his hand and stepped out of the car.

"Thank you for the ride," Imani said, smiling. She had just met Derrick at the grocery store and figured she would save the Uber fare and allow him to bring her home. He didn't know it, but he was going to serve more than one purpose today. Carlton had been acting funny and very dismissive toward her lately. She needed him to recognize that he wasn't the only one with other options.

"You are more than welcome for the ride," he responded.

Imani placed her key in the front door. "I'm glad you were there, too. Come on inside. Can I get you something to drink?" She placed her purse on the table in the foyer and walked to the kitchen. Derrick followed her as he looked around the rooms. They walked into the large kitchen, and Imani walked over to the sink and began washing her hands.

"Okay, let's see what we have here," she said, opening the refrigerator. Imani was a beautiful girl, and Derrick was actually seeing her in her natural state. Her hair was in a messy ponytail, she wore no makeup, and she was in simple leggings and a T-shirt. She sighed as she took two glasses from the cabinet and filled them with ice.

"So we have a choice of ginger ale, orange juice, or sweet tea," Imani said, laughing.

"Tea sounds good to me." Derrick sat down on the black barstool. Yogi entered the kitchen, carrying Caleb.

"Jesus!" Yogi screamed, holding her chest. "I didn't hear anyone come in."

Caleb cooed and giggled when he saw his mother and began reaching for her. She took the baby from Yogi and smelled Caleb and covered him with kisses. Seeing, holding, and smelling him made her realize how much she needed to make sure he had a full-time father in his life whether it was his real father, Carlton, or not.

"He feels like he needs to be changed. Excuse me a second. We will be right back." Imani left the kitchen.

Yogi and Derrick made small talk while they sat and enjoyed a cold beverage.

"Well, he is dry and happy now," Imani announced, coming back into the room. Carlton opened the patio door, and Imani's body tensed as Carlton entered the kitchen.

"Hey, babe. Hey, Mani, how's my godson?" Carlton asked, walking over to Imani and Caleb.

"He's great. Thanks to his mommy and Derrick, he's about to have some lunch," Imani said, smiling over at Derrick.

"Well, Imani and Derrick, I guess we are grateful to you," Carlton responded, kissed Imani's forehead, and hit Derrick with a slight bow.

Imani's body tingled as Carlton's lips pressed against her forehead. There was a time when all she wanted to do was lie up and make love to him, and now she was confused as fuck. Part of her wanted him and part just wanted to know that she could have him.

"Well, I should get going. I still have a few errands to run," Derrick said, standing.

"We will walk you out," Imani suggested, tightening her grip on Caleb.

"You know, if you're up to it, y'all can roll with me. We could grab a bite to eat instead of you having to make y'all something," Derrick said, smiling and shaking Caleb's foot.

"I don't think your car is made for a toddler." Imani laughed.

"Well, I'll go home and get a car that is suitable."

Imani blushed. "No need to do all that. Next time though for sure." She smiled and raised Caleb's hand to wave to him.

Carlton was looking out the front door window. He couldn't understand the feelings he was having at the moment. Seeing Imani interact with another dude and thoughts of her taking his son stirred up feelings of jealousy in him. He should be happy her needy ass had her attention on someone else, but the truth was it was pissing him the fuck off.

King was leaving the office, headed out to his car. He knew that a successful record label would take his bank account to new legal heights, but wrapping up in the game and running a business was a lot. He was constantly switching from the office to the streets, and it was beginning to take a toll on him. In addition to all of that, he still had to show support for Kareem. The man had lost the mother of his children, and he was out here juggling fatherhood with grieving and trying to find the people responsible for Tiana's death.

"King? May I have a word with you?"

King turned around and saw one of the detectives working Tiana's case approaching him. King loved Tiana like a sister, but because of who he was and how he made his money, the sight of any kind of law enforcement made his skin crawl. He didn't need to get jammed up because of anyone else's actions, but he also didn't want to come across as uncooperative. He wanted to get his hands on whoever was responsible for putting that bomb underneath Imani's car, but he had to let the police think he wanted justice the old-fashioned way. As the detective neared him, a thought entered his mind.

"Hi, sorry to bother you, but I'm still looking into the Tiana Branch case, and I wanted to know if maybe anything else had crossed your mind that could help us," the young white detective said.

King hated the fact that most times when cases did get solved it was because of information given to the police and not from them doing a good job on their own. He had never been one to fuck with the police, but just maybe they might be able to find out some things that he couldn't.

"All I know is that the bomb was under Imani Ross's car, which means it was meant for her. Tiana was only in the car because it was blocking hers. So, maybe you should be asking Ms. Ross who might want her dead. Maybe start with her child's father," King hinted before turning his back on the officer. That was as much of someone else's job that he was going to do for today.

Chapter Five

Carlton opened his front door and frowned when he saw two detectives headed in his direction. He had just gotten off the phone with Panama discussing how much money they were losing daily because of this street war. He was not in the mood for any questions. Whether the detectives were there concerning him or not, he had a disdain for the police, and he didn't like them showing up at his home unannounced.

"Good morning, sir. I'm Detective Baker, and this is my partner, Detective Johnson. We were informed that Ms. Imani Ross is currently living here. Is she available? We'd like a word with her regarding the murder investigation of Mrs. Tiana Branch."

If nothing else, Carlton had become a great actor. Especially with his mistress and their child living under the same roof as him and his wife. "No, she's not. I slept in this morning and woke up to an empty house, but I'll be sure to tell her that you gentlemen came by."

"Thank you. Oh, one quick question, I know Ms. Ross has a young child. By any chance has she ever mentioned who the father is, or has he ever come by? Maybe she mentioned them having a strained relationship or something?"

Carlton did his best to look as if he was trying to recall ever hearing Imani mention anything about the man she had a child with. "I can't really recall ever hearing her mention anything about her baby's father. But honestly

Imani saves all of the girl talk for my wife and daughter. She and my daughter are best friends, and that's how she became close with our family. When my wife found out the young girl was expecting and down on her luck, we didn't hesitate to open our home up to her. I can say that, to my knowledge, she has never had any male company here."

Detective Baker tipped his head at Carlton. "Thank you for your time, sir. Please give Ms. Ross my card and have her reach out to me. I'd like to get this case wrapped up and give Mrs. Branch's family some closure."

Carlton took the card and abandoned his plans of leaving the house. He headed back upstairs to the room that Imani occupied. He hadn't been truthful with the detectives. He had woken up an hour ago to Yogi saying that she had an errand to run, and Imani was in the room with Caleb. Carlton wasn't sure why he told the detectives that he was home alone, but he was glad that he had. He tapped lightly on Imani's door.

"Come in."

When Carlton entered the room, he noticed that Imani tensed up. She was sitting in a rocking chair, rocking Caleb and feeding him. The fact that she tensed up meant that he had her on the right path and had done a good job of making her regret playing with him. Not aborting Caleb, moving in his house with him and Yogi, she really felt she had him by the balls, but hopefully now she was understanding he was not to be fucked with. But just in case she needed a little more convincing, Carlton was going to place the cherry on top.

"The police just left here," he spoke while handing Imani the card that the detective left behind. "Seems they are hell-bent on solving this case with Tiana, and they are looking at people who might want you dead. Namely, they want to know who the father of your child is. Now I suggest that you lie to them, and I have the perfect person to give them. Red was one of Kareem's and King's biggest rivals. So, it would make sense as to how the bomb ended up underneath your car. This would also confirm for Kareem that indeed it was his enemies responsible for the death of his wife, making him and King go harder to end this problem."

Imani looked down at her son, then up at Carlton. "Yeah, how did a bomb end up underneath my car? Since we're looking at my baby daddy as a suspect, then only he can tell me the answer," she stated bravely.

A sinister grin covered Carlton's face. He cupped Imani's chin in his hand and squeezed tightly. "You're a very lucky young lady. One might even say that you have nine lives. The fact that you played in my face one too many times and you're still breathing, that alone is something that you should get down on your knees and thank God for. You moved your little ass into my home with my wife, and you paraded your pregnant belly in her face like the shit was a game. True, I was wrong for sleeping with you, but you've gone above and beyond to play games and take my and Yogi's kindness for weakness. I'm done with the bullshit. What you will do is find an apartment and move out of this house. I will pay the rent for six months, and after that, you will get a job. I will take care of my child, but I will not take care of your li'l ass. And if you even think of going to my wife and telling her anything, I will make sure that this time it won't be a bomb or quick death awaiting you. Do you understand me?"

Carlton didn't wait for her to respond. He shook her head yes for her. Bending down, he kissed Caleb on the head and turned and left the room.

A shiver ran down Imani's spine. In the back of her mind, she always felt that it was him. Now she knew for sure, and she couldn't stop shaking. Imani gazed down into her son's big, bright eyes. She didn't even realize that she was crying until a tear dripped off her chin and fell onto Caleb's romper. She had indeed played games with Carlton. She had even done as he said and played in Yogi's face. That woman had been such a help to her, and if she had any idea that Carlton was Caleb's father, she might do bodily harm to the both of them. Things had gone left way too quick. Imani had allowed herself to fall for and be manipulated by an older, married man. Looking down at her son, there was no way that she could regret not aborting him, but she had put them in this situation and now had to get them out of it.

Kareem looked at his ringing cell phone and ignored the call. Stressed wasn't the word. He woke up every day missing Tiana. He woke up to his kids missing Tiana and not understanding why their mother was gone. He had been so consumed with grief that he was looking in all the wrong places for answers. When the detectives told him they were focusing on Imani's baby father, he figured he would do the same. Imani was a friend of the family, and he didn't blame her or want her to feel intimidated, so he asked her to pick Keana up from school. That would give him a chance to be around her and ask a few questions. KJ was in his room playing a game, and Kordell had gone to an after-school program. Each of his kids was dealing with missing their mother in their own way, and whatever it was, he let them. Kareem heard someone coming on the porch of the home.

The door opened, and Keana stepped inside of the house with a smile on her face, holding an ice cream cone, and Imani was close behind her. "Daddy, Imani got me ice cream."

"I hope that's okay," Imani stated.

Kareem's eyes didn't leave Keana's face as he gave her a genuine smile. "It's whatever you want, baby girl. Give me a few moments to talk to Ms. Imani, and then you can tell me about your day at school."

"Okay." Keana headed for her room, and Kareem gave Imani his attention.

"Thank you for picking her up."

"It was no problem. I was out anyway. I'm thinking of getting my own place, so I went to view some apartments. I also need to get a job." She looked away for a moment. Kareem could tell those were things that she didn't really want to be doing, and her son was still young.

"Something going on at Yogi and Carlton's place?"

Imani looked back at him. Kareem was fine as hell. Always had been fine to her, and he may have stepped out on Tiana from time to time for all she knew, but he would have never cheated with her being so close to the family. She knew this, but Tiana was no more. She hated to seem so cold and callous, but she had to think about Caleb. If Carlton was going to pay her rent for a period of time, that would be a big help, but she didn't want to have to spend forty hours a week away from her son once that was over. She knew the fastest way to get money was to be affiliated with a get-money nigga, and Kareem was it. His home was absolutely gorgeous, and he had three kids he needed help with. If she could get on his good side, maybe they could be the answer to each other's problems. Or at least most of them.

"Yes, everything is fine. I just think that Yogi and Carlton have been more than kind to me, and I want to give them their space back. It's not their fault that I had a baby by a deadbeat and I'm in this thing alone. I have to try to be independent as much as I can and fix the mess that I made."

Kareem was glad she brought it up so he wouldn't have to. "Speaking of Caleb's father, who is he anyway? I mean, the nigga really put a bomb under your car? I've never seen a baby mama–baby daddy relationship go that fucking hard."

Imani's body hardened. If only he knew that it was Carlton. What would he do then? Maybe he would get rid of him and part of her problems would be solved? But then she thought about it. Maybe he wouldn't believe her and tell Carlton, and she would surely end up dead. Instead, Imani blurted out the name that Carlton had given her. "His name is Red."

Kareem frowned. "This entire time you were dealing with and had a baby by sorry-ass Red?" He couldn't hide his disdain if he wanted to.

"I . . . no." Imani began to stumble over her words. "It wasn't like that. It was just some drunk, sneaky link shit a few times, and the condom broke. By the time I found out I was pregnant, I was kind of far along, and I didn't want to get an abortion because I don't believe in that. He didn't want me to have it and got angry, and I guess you know the rest." She looked down shamefully. "I didn't know about y'all beef until after I was already pregnant. I swear."

Kareem studied Imani for a bit. He was Muslim and didn't believe in abortion either and would never tell a woman to have one. Red was a sorry, grimy-ass nigga, and this sounded just like some shit he would do. Even though he was dead, somebody was still going to pay for Tiana's death. He knew Red wouldn't have placed the bomb on the car himself. So now he would be turning his attention to the culprit and everyone affiliated with Red. They all were about to be wiped off the face of the fucking earth.

"It's okay, Imani. I know you didn't mean for any of this shit to happen," Kareem responded while pulling her in for an embrace.

Imani ramped up her crying and tightened her hug on Kareem. He consoled her for nearly two minutes in his arms before releasing her.

"Did you find any apartments that you like?" he asked, trying to ease the tension.

"Out of the three that I viewed, I really liked the first one the best. I'm going back to apply tomorrow."

"That's what's up. I'm sure you will get it, and let me know if there's anything I can do to help. Here." He stood up and dug in his pocket. "Let me give you gas money for picking Keana up."

"Oh, no, you don't have to do that. It wasn't too far, and I have a full tank. Besides I can help you with the kids whenever you want. I love being around them," she stated eagerly. "And I know it has to be hard on you. Picking them up, dropping them off, babysitting. I can do all of it, until I find a job, that is."

"I appreciate that, and I will keep it in mind. Thank you again, but please take this gas money. It's nothing, and cars don't run off water."

Imani smiled and took the money from Kareem.

"Bye, Reem. Please tell the kids Aunt Imani said good-bye and their cousin Caleb would love to see them soon."

By the time she got in her vehicle, Imani had made up her mind that she would definitely be working on getting closer to Kareem.

Chapter Six

King walked into the family room of Yogi and Carlton's home with Sloan and Merrick by his side. Khristian, Imani, Yogi, and Carlton were all seated. King eyed Caleb, who was sitting on his mother's lap babbling playfully. Sloan spoke to everyone in the room and took a seat next to Yogi. She felt like shit, and she had decided that she needed to go ahead and make a doctor's appointment. She knew people who had gotten food poisoning and had suffered for a few days, but she was starting to become concerned. Her schedule was really about to pick up, and she needed to be on her A game.

Yogi eyed Sloan dressed in a black silk wrap dress that clung to her body, and she smiled inwardly. The woman had grown on her for certain, and she now liked Sloan for her son. King cleared his throat and got everyone's attention.

"I know we all have things to do, so I will make this quick. This is Merrick. Expect to see a lot of him. He's an old friend of Panama's. This war with the other side is getting thick. We lost Tiana, and I'm not trying to lose anyone else. Carlton, I know you may want to have your own security around the house, but Merrick is here to watch over this family until further notice. We all need to play it safe." He directed his attention to Khristian. "Of course, he can't follow you back to college. But when you are in town and need to hit up the mall, the grocery store, anywhere out in public, he will accompany you then.

Same goes for Mommy and Imani. Now, we know he can't be everywhere at once, so I'm asking you all, until this is finished, try to limit your time outside."

King expected a lot of grumbling, and he was surprised when there was none. Maybe the bomb in Imani's car and Tiana's untimely death had really spooked everyone. He was handling things the best he knew how, but wiping out an entire crew would take time.

"Any questions?" he asked for clarity.

"So, we like have to call and get permission before we go somewhere?" Khristian asked.

"Not necessarily permission, but you will make Merrick aware of where you would like to go and when, and he will drive you and accompany you." King looked around the room, and when no one said anything else, he nodded his head. "That's all for now."

Khristian walked over to Imani and picked the baby up off her lap, and Yogi walked over to Merrick and King. This was a stressful time for her family, but Yogi was still human, and her eyes still worked. Merrick appeared slightly younger than her, and his muscular build and salt-and-pepper curls were two attributes that made him very easy on the eyes.

"I'm Yogi," she extended her hand and introduced herself. "I'm King's mother."

"How are you doing, Yogi?" Merrick was poised and professional. His tone was polite, but he didn't even smile. Yet, the way his eyes were locked with Yogi's had Carlton staring from across the room.

Kareem called King's phone, and he excused himself to answer. "What's up, fam?" he asked as he stepped onto the porch.

"Yo, I talked to Imani yesterday, and something with shorty's story isn't adding up. She told me that Caleb's father is Red."

King frowned up his face. "What? Red?" He thought back to the conversations he'd had with Yogi about Imani's situation, and he had been told that Imani was pregnant by an older, married man who didn't want the baby. Maybe Red was older than her, but they made it seem like this cat was way older than Imani. In addition to that, Red had bitches, but he wasn't married.

"That's what she said. She said it wasn't anything serious and that they only fucked around a few times. Her dealing with Red isn't far-fetched, but didn't you say that her baby daddy was married?"

"That's the story that she gave Carlton and Yogi. Maybe she was just embarrassed to admit that she was pregnant by him, especially after it became known that we were beefing with them." King was trying to make sense of the news that he'd just been hit with.

"I don't know what the issue is, but I don't need shorty being embarrassed and keeping secrets or withholding information. Tiana shouldn't have died, and I'm not going to rest until I get to the bottom of this shit. I don't care how many bodies have to drop."

King knew that Kareem was as serious as a heart attack and rightfully so. "Patience, my brother. It's going to happen soon enough." Sloan came outside and stood by King's side.

He was almost sorry that he had brought her into his world. A woman like her didn't fit into all this madness, but here she was right by his side. King ended the call and gazed into Sloan's eyes. "Talk to me."

"I just wanted to come make sure you were okay."

King kissed Sloan on the forehead. No matter how good of a role he tried to play, she could feel the stress oozing off of him, and she was worried about him. Sloan wasn't dumb, and she knew the things he was into were potentially dangerous for him and those around him, but she still couldn't walk away. She knew there were certain things he'd never let her see, but his kiss and the way he wrapped his arms around her made her feel like he had everything under control.

"I'm more than okay. What about you? You've been looking pale lately. Are you able to handle the schedule that we laid out for you?"

Sloan didn't feel like herself. She felt sluggish and tired, but she refused to let on just how tired she was. Her career was something that she'd been praying for, and a little case of a stomach bug or food poisoning wasn't going to set her back. Sloan decided that she would go to the doctor and, if needed, get an IV or anything necessary to put nutrients back in her body and get her to 100 percent.

It was her turn to smile and assure King. "The schedule that I have is fine. I just need a little power nap, and I'll be A1."

"Let's get you home then."

"If you need to go somewhere, I can take you," Carlton said to Yogi as she sat at her vanity putting cream on her face. Carlton came in when Yogi was getting ready for bed, and she was surprised. Most nights, he didn't make it in until after she was asleep. It was yet another thing that Yogi was used to that she didn't concern herself too much with these days. She felt she was just dealing with her marriage and not stressing the things that she couldn't change, but Carlton knew it was more than that. A man can sense when a woman has removed her emotions from the equation.

Yogi eyed him through the mirror of the vanity. "Since when do you have time to chauffeur me around?"

Carlton could have retired a long time ago if he didn't spend so much money hoing, and now Kareem's insistence on waging war with all of Charlotte was making all of them dig into their savings. But even with that, he still had a nice income set up for him and Yogi. He could have spent his days playing golf, reading, or other small things to pass the time. She wasn't asking for that, but he damn sure didn't have to be out nearly as much as he was, and he for sure didn't have to stay out until all hours of the morning. Yogi was no fool. She knew Carlton was out cheating most nights when he wasn't home with her. She wasn't sure why he had a sudden interest in taking her places, but then it hit her. He didn't want Merrick taking her. This nigga had a nerve to be jealous.

Carlton sighed. "Why do you have to fight me and question me on everything? If I said I can take you, then I can take you."

Yogi ignored his statement. "Have you talked to Imani? She said she's moving out, and I just don't understand why. She doesn't even have a job yet, and she still needs help with Caleb. I don't think it's a good idea, but she said she found a place. Maybe you should talk to her. If we both make her feel welcome, maybe she'll change her mind about leaving."

"Make her feel welcome? Isn't that what we've been doing? That girl is grown and has a mind of her own. Living here with us probably feels like living with her parents. If she wants her freedom and privacy, let her have it."

Yogi scoffed but remained quiet. She enjoyed having Caleb in the house. Imani and Caleb being there was better than it just being her and Carlton. When they left, she'd once again be alone most of the time, and even when Carlton was in the home, sometimes she still felt alone. There were instances where they were in the same house for hours and they didn't say ten words to each other. Yogi stood up, and Carlton took a few steps until they were face-to-face. He grabbed his wife's hands and looked into her eyes.

"This is our time. You said you didn't want any more kids. Fine. We can travel more. We can relax more. We can sit back and enjoy life. We can fall in love with each other all over again and remember why we got married in the first place."

Yogi stared at him with a blank expression on her face. If that's all it took for Carlton to finally see her and put forth an effort to make their marriage work, she would have gotten an attractive driver years ago. Yogi realized that her husband was waiting on a response, and she didn't have the desire to be up half the night arguing. "Sure, dear. We can do that." Yogi gave Carlton a tight smile and walked around him to get in bed.

Carlton looked over his shoulder at his wife. He could sense it. Yogi was finally tired of his shit.

Chapter Seven

Sloan observed her nails while she waited in the room for the doctor to come in. She was anxious to get some kind of diagnosis or recommendation from her doctor because whatever she wanted to do, she would do it. If she had to take vitamins, get an IV to hydrate, change her diet . . . anything to feel better. She had a busy few weeks ahead, and Sloan wanted her energy back. She was trying to mentally figure out when she'd have time for a manicure when there was a light knock on the door.

"Come in," she called out.

The middle-aged Indian doctor walked into the room with a smile on her face. Sloan had been going to her for the past four years, and she liked the woman. "Hellooooo," the doctor sang out and took a seat on a stool with Sloan's chart in her hand. "How are we doing?"

"We are extremely tired, and my stomach has been on go lately. Some days, I have cramps. I've dealt with nausea, vomiting, and some days, I have this full, bloated feeling. It all started after I ate some crab legs, so I'm thinking I might have food poisoning."

Dr. Saida smiled at Sloan. "My dear, you don't have food poisoning. You are pregnant. You told the nurse that your last period was more than three weeks ago. We don't have anything in your chart about irregular periods. Did you notice that you were late?"

Sloan was stunned. "Um, I . . ." She racked her brain, trying to figure out why she hadn't noticed that her cycle was so late. "I have been late a few times in the past. There were even a few times that my period didn't come, or it only lasted a day or two, but I was on birth control, and I knew I wasn't pregnant. I chalked it up to stress or just a change in my cycle. I was on birth control for six years, so even though I made the choice to give my body a break from it, I'm still used to the effects that birth control had on my cycle. So, no, pregnancy hadn't crossed my mind."

"It can definitely be hard to pay attention to those things when you were on birth control for so long, but remember when you came to me about getting off and I told you that unless you wanted a baby, you needed to be careful?"

"I remember," Sloan mumbled in a low tone. She couldn't believe that she had been so careless. She blinked back tears as the doctor stood up. Her career was finally about to take off, and she was pregnant? Sloan felt naive as hell because pregnancy was literally the last thing that she thought about. She had enough going on, and to add to the situation, King was in a whole war. There was no way she needed a baby right now. So, she was going to turn into one of those women who had an abortion because a baby would hurt her career? Sloan was truly disappointed in herself.

The doctor gave Sloan a vaginal exam and then she did a vaginal ultrasound. Sloan's own heart began to pump wildly when sounds of her child's heartbeat filled the room. She clearly knew nothing about being pregnant because she was stunned that her child had a heartbeat that could be heard so clearly this early in the pregnancy. Her stomach was still flat as a board. Sloan tried to process everything that the doctor was saying, but there were too many thoughts running rampant in her mind. It felt as if she floated out of the doctor's office. As if she were having an out-of-body experience, Sloan made it home without even remembering how. She was supposed to get her prescription for prenatal vitamins and iron pills filled, but she forgot. Would they help her to feel any better? She doubted it. Fatigue seemed to be a universal symptom of pregnancy, and that was something that she didn't have time for.

Sloan's phone rang, snapping her from her daze. King was calling. He was sure to ask her how the doctor's appointment went, and she wasn't sure she wanted to tell him. If he was in his right mind, he'd agree that this wasn't the time to have a baby, and he would fully back her decision to have an abortion, but what if he wanted the baby? That thought was enough to scare Sloan into not answering the phone for King.

"Hey, girl," Donna heard someone call out. She looked over her shoulder and smiled at Imani coming toward her with a baby strapped to the front of her body in one of those carriers.

"Hey! I didn't know you had a baby. He is too cute!" Donna walked around so she could see Caleb's face. A lot of people deemed her to simply be a hood rat because she liked to play the hood, she had ghetto friends, and she was known to rock colored wigs, but Donna was actually very smart, and she knew Imani from a class they took together their freshman year of college.

"Thank you, and he is a handful!" Imani peeped that Donna was loaded down with bags. "Somebody's tearing the mall down, I see."

Donna giggled. "This new nigga I'm talking to. He's cool or whatever. Came a li'l heavy with the tricking, and I don't turn down no paper."

"I know that's right," Imani gushed, but she felt a tinge of jealousy. She remembered when Carlton used to finance all of her shopping sprees and give her large amounts of money to blow. Imani looked down at Caleb. She loved her son, but keeping him had backfired. She and Carlton didn't end up together, and she now had to figure out how she was going to take care of them.

"I know you're a new mommy and all, but we have to link sometimes. I'm always down to go out, and if you can't hit the club, then we can go out for lunch or something."

Nothing had changed, and Imani knew that the club was one of the best places to find a baller. She was sure that she could get Yogi to babysit. Especially since she had signed the lease on a new place, and she would be moving out soon. Even though he said he wasn't going to take care of her, Carlton was nice enough to promise her money for furniture and the first six months' rent. All she would have to worry about were the utilities. For now. Imani still had it, and she knew she could finesse a nigga. She'd been texting Derrick, and he was cool, too. At this point, Imani was willing to date as many men as she had to until she found the one who would meet her financial needs.

"Girl, I could definitely use a night out. Let's exchange numbers. I love my son, but Mama gotta have a life, too."

The women exchanged numbers, and unbeknownst to them, Texas and his homie Ron were coming out of a store a few feet away. Texas had given Donna money to come to the mall and decided that he needed a few things himself, so he scooped Ron and they came out to shop.

Ron was always on the prowl for a new female to hit even though he was engaged. "Who is that Donna is talking to?" He rubbed his hands anxiously, already anticipating asking Donna to put him down with the beauty.

Texas smirked. "Oh, that's the infamous Imani. Her name has been ringing bells for a few days now."

Ron looked over at him curiously. "Why? Who is she?" It wasn't often that he was out of the loop on hood gossip.

"Police came to Red's mom's house talking about did she know that Red had a kid. Of course, she said no, and she got to calling around asking people about who this Imani chick was. It even got back to Peaches. I didn't know Donna knew the broad, but it works in my favor, especially since she's affiliated with that nigga King. Now, it's possible that Red hit that, made a baby, and didn't tell anyone. Or it's possible that she could be lying. If that's Red's seed, she gets a pass, but if it's not"—he glared at Imani—"that bitch is gonna be swimming with the fishes."

Imani headed out to her car already plotting. She would get Yogi to babysit at least twice a week while she went out and tried to put a plan in motion. She buckled the baby in, and her cell phone rang just as she was getting in the car. Imani smirked when she saw Kareem's name on her screen. "Hey, Kareem, what's up?"

"What's up, Imani? I hate to hit you on short notice, but Keana's teacher called and said she was running a fever, and I'm like an hour and thirty minutes outside the city. Are you able to go get her for me? She has a key in her bookbag, so she'll be able to let you in the crib."

A sinister grin crossed Imani's face. "Sure, I can do that. I'm not far from her school."

Kareem breathed a sigh of relief. "You're a lifesaver. I really appreciate it."

"You don't have to thank me, Reem. I told you, anytime I could help with the kids, I will. I'm on my way right now."

Imani ended the call with Kareem and did a little dance in her seat. "Looks like things are finally starting to come together for me. In a minute, I won't need Carlton's petty-ass money." She looked over her shoulder into the back seat and stared into her son's big, round eyes. "Give Mommy a few weeks, baby boy, and you're going to have a new daddy. Carlton's old ass ain't stopping shit."

King entered the room where Sloan was closed up in the booth, recording. He nodded his head at the engineer and watched as she did her thing. Sloan was so into the song that she was singing that she didn't even notice he had come into the room until she was done. She hung the headphones up and stepped out of the booth. King could tell that his presence had her nervous, and he wondered what was up with her all of a sudden. Had this new situation made her realize that they came from two different worlds, and maybe his street life was too much for her? He couldn't blame her if she had come to that realization, but she could at least be honest with him and not leave him in the dark. King had called her three times, and she had yet to answer or call him back, and that wasn't like her.

"Hey, my man, can we get a minute alone?" King asked the engineer.

"Sure thing." The engineer left the room, and Sloan still couldn't make eye contact with King. "What's good with you, *mami?*" he asked her. If she was starting to get cold feet because of his lifestyle, he was prepared to try to make her understand that he would do whatever he could to keep her safe.

"I'm pregnant." Sloan's eyes were everywhere except on his face.

Her words stunned King. She was having a baby? He stared at Sloan for so long that she finally looked at him. She had already been nervous about his response, and his silence wasn't making it any better. "You're pregnant, and you didn't say anything to me?" he finally spoke.

"I was just really trying to process it. I was on birth control for years. I can't believe I allowed myself to be so careless. But I think we can both agree that this isn't a good time for a child."

"What do you mean this isn't a good time for a child? We have nine months to prepare, right? That's almost a year. I think by the time the baby comes we'll be good."

"We'll be good?" Sloan asked with a confused expression on her face. "King, if I work every day, my album might be done in a month. We're looking at nonstop travel and promo for the album during the first few months of my pregnancy when I'd be sick and tired all of the time. I just don't think it's a good idea."

"Look at you now. You're in the booth, and you're working. This isn't fifteen years ago. You know how many female artists have kids now and are still hot? Cardi B has announced both of her pregnancies on national TV during performances. You don't have to go the Beyoncé route. You don't have to wait until your career has taken off to have kids. Trust me."

"Trust you? How do you know, King? Have you ever been pregnant and had to hop on and off planes or get on stage and perform or get up at four in the morning to do radio or had to stand up for hours at a time for a photo shoot while pregnant?" A man standing in her face telling her what she could do while she was pregnant was irritating her. Sloan had been in the studio for three hours, and the entire time, she'd been fighting the urge to throw up. She just wanted to lie down and take a fifteen-minute nap. Sloan saluted any woman who could stand on stage and perform and drop it like it was hot with a big belly because she didn't even have the strength to do that now, and she wasn't even showing.

"So you want to get an abortion?" King actually looked hurt, and Sloan couldn't believe that as the owner of the label and a drug kingpin currently involved in an all-out street war, he was really encouraging her to have a child.

"I just think it would be best, baby."

King dropped his head. He had spent thousands of dollars on abortions over the years, so it wasn't like this would be his first. But truthfully he thought all that was behind him. He loved Sloan and wanted a family with her. In the past it was him hoping that the female didn't want the child, but now the table had changed, and he didn't like the feeling.

"I guess you have to do what you think is best," he whispered lightly before turning and walking away, leaving Sloan standing there looking helpless and defeated.

He had just told her she could get the abortion if she wanted, but Sloan couldn't feel good about it. Instead she actually felt guilty. Was she being selfish for wanting to choose her career over being a mother right now? Not to mention not wanting a child in the middle of a drug war. His family couldn't even leave the house without protection, and he really thought having a child would be a good idea? *Look at what almost happened with Imani.* Sloan got chills when she thought about the fact that Imani and her child could have been in that truck rather than Tiana. No, she couldn't do it. Sloan couldn't bring a baby into the chaos that was her and King's world. As soon as she left the studio, she was going to schedule an abortion.

Chapter Eight

"Do you want something to eat?" Imani asked Keana in a syrupy sweet voice after they entered the house. Caleb was asleep, so Imani placed his carrier on the floor in the living room.

"No, I just want to get in my bed," Keana stated in a small voice.

"Okay. Well, come on and let me tuck you in. I'll look in the kitchen and see if your dad has some soup or something so if you do get hungry, you can eat. Okay?"

Keana nodded, and Imani followed her up the stairs to her bedroom. Once Keana was snug in bed, Imani pulled the covers up over her. "I'm not going anywhere until your dad gets here, so if you want something to drink or if you need anything, just holler out and let me know."

Keana nodded, and Imani left the room. She headed straight for the kitchen to see what Kareem had. He and his kids were living in a gorgeous house, and Imani could see herself and Caleb moving in with them and making it a real home. They could be one big, happy family. Imani smiled as she pulled a pack of chicken out of the freezer. She hopefully had time to thaw the chicken out and whip up a meal for Kareem and the kids. She needed to show him that she could be an asset.

Imani moved around the kitchen like she lived there, pulling contents out of the cabinets and the fridge. Once she saw what Kareem was working with, she decided on baked chicken, macaroni and cheese, and green beans.

That was a simple enough meal that hopefully his kids would like. Imani walked into the living room to check on her sleeping child, and it was right back to the kitchen to start dinner. She knew she had to be subtle. Kareem was still grieving, so she couldn't come right out and try to sleep with him. It would have been tacky. He was still human though, and if she put herself in his direct line of vision often enough, once he got horny, she would hopefully be on his radar.

When Kareem entered the house forty-five minutes later, he saw Imani sitting on his couch feeding Caleb, and the smell of food lingered in the air.

"Thanks for getting Keana for me, Mani. I really appreciate that. You cookin' something?" he asked, wondering if he was tripping, but somethin' damn sure smelled like chicken.

"Yes. You had some chicken in the freezer, so I took it out. That way you wouldn't have to worry about feeding the kids when you got here."

"Oh, word? I appreciate that. I'm starving my damn self, but the other kids are with Tiana's mom. They'll be here later. Where is Keana? How is she?"

Imani peeped the concern on his face. "She's asleep. I just looked in on her a few minutes ago. She said she's not hungry. I think you should make an appointment to take her to the doctor in the morning just to make sure she's good. I gave her some Tylenol, and it broke her fever, but it's always better to be safe and not sorry."

Kareem breathed a sigh of relief and sat down on the couch. "Damn, man. I didn't even think about stopping to get Tylenol. I'm glad there was some already here. Tiana usually handled that shit. I'm really out here trying to juggle three kids by myself, and I don't know what the hell I'm doing," Kareem admitted sadly, and Imani felt bad for him.

She was too young to be tied down with four kids, but at least Kareem didn't have super small babies. The older ones could do a lot for themselves, and Imani was focused on the bigger picture. If she had to play stepmother to some kids in order to have stability for her and her son, that was the sacrifice that she would have to make. When she spoke, she made sure her tone was soothing and reassuring.

"It's okay, Reem. You'll be fine. You have me, and the kids' grandmother, and you know Yogi will always help. You have a lot of support, and we are all happy to help you."

Kareem looked over at Imani. "Thank you. I appreciate that. I'm about to look in on Keana. Is the food ready?"

"Not quite. The chicken has about another hour, but the sides are done. When I'm done feeding Caleb, I'll get out of your hair and be on my way."

Kareem stood and pulled some money from his pocket. "You saved my life, and there's no need to tell me that I don't have to pay you. Time is money, and you have given up your time to help me with my child."

He passed Imani the money, and she smiled at him just as Kordell and KJ burst through the door with Tiana's mother close behind. "Is Keana okay?" she asked with concern before her eyes fell on Imani, and she raised one eyebrow.

Imani smiled nervously and busied herself with burping Caleb and wiping his mouth.

"She's upstairs asleep. I wasn't nearby when the school called, so I asked Imani to go get her for me. She's—"

Tiana's mother cut her off. "I know who she is. She's the woman who is supposed to be dead instead of my daughter."

The woman's voice was so cold that a chill ran through Imani's body. She placed her son in his carrier and was going to leave before she had to curse that old bitch out.

Kareem shook his head. "That wasn't necessary. She had nothing to do with a bomb being placed in her car. Nobody should be dead but the fuck niggas who did what they did."

As mad as she was, it still made Imani feel good to hear Kareem defending her. Tiana's bitch of a mother didn't respond. She didn't even attempt to apologize. She just walked up the stairs so she could go check on Keana.

"I'm sorry about that. That was out of pocket for real," Kareem apologized.

"It's fine." Imani stood up and picked the carrier up without making eye contact. She was furious and embarrassed.

"Imani," Kareem called firmly, making her look up at him. "She was wrong and rude for that shit, and you were the bigger person for not being rude back to her. Thank you."

Imani choked back tears and nodded. The way that Kareem was staring at her made her feel better, and little did that old bat know that she had just helped Imani out. Kareem being all caring with her would hopefully work in her favor. Sooner rather than later, she'd be riding Kareem's face and raising Tiana's kids, and she hoped it made that old bitch have a heart attack.

"You're welcome. I'm going to get Caleb home. Tell Keana I hope she feels better."

As soon as the door closed behind her, a smile graced Imani's face. Things were definitely going according to plan.

"King! What is wrong with you?" Yogi stared at her son. "I have been talking to you for the past ten minutes, and you aren't listening to a thing I said." Yogi and King were sitting in the living room of her home, and he was preoccupied with thoughts of Sloan. They hadn't spoken since the day before.

King made eye contact with his mother. "I'm sorry. I just got a lot on my mind. What did you say?"

Yogi gave him a knowing look. "Boy, don't play with me. The fact that you have something on your mind is obvious. I'm waiting for you to tell me what it is."

Yogi knew King like the back of her own hand, and she was far from dumb. King knew that it wouldn't be easy to get anything over on her, but he didn't want to tell her that Sloan was pregnant. Yogi was the queen of doing too much, and she'd go straight to Sloan and put her two cents in, and King didn't want that. His and Sloan's opinion were the only opinions that mattered, and at this point he wasn't even sure how much his mattered. It was Sloan's body, and she seemed to be against having a baby. If she did abort his child, King wasn't sure how he could move forward with her. He didn't care what the reasons were. He didn't agree with it, and he wouldn't pretend like he did. In his mind it was possible for her to have a child and a career. Sloan was being unnecessarily selfish. However, King wasn't in the mood to get into all of that with Yogi today.

"I just have a lot on my mind. Seeing what Kareem is going through, never knowing who might be next or when . . . I'm just ready to wrap all of this beef shit up and focus on other things. That's all, Ma." He hoped she bought his story.

Yogi gave her son a sympathetic look, and King could tell that she had. "Son, you know I hate to see you stressed. But I also know the man you are, and I know you will come out on top. I have no doubt in my mind about that. Just focus and don't let anyone or anything knock you off your game."

King thought that was a funny statement because the issue with Sloan was threatening to do just that. He finished up lunch with his mother and decided that he would head to the office. Yogi watched her son leave, and then she called Merrick.

"Peace and blessing. What's going on?" Merrick answered the phone on the first ring. King was paying him good money to be on point, and that was what he was.

"Hello, Merrick. I hate to bother you on such short notice, but I need to run a few errands. It shouldn't take more than an hour or two. Would you be able to assist me?" Yogi knew that Carlton's ass was all talk. Before he left the house most days, he didn't even bother to ask her if she had anything that she needed to do.

"Sure thing. I'll be there in about fifteen minutes."

"Thank you."

Yogi stared out of the window at her massive lawn. She couldn't help but to worry while wondering what would become of this situation with King. Yogi was involved in the game for many years by way of the men she chose to deal with and now by her only son being a part of it. In some ways, she was used to this life, but as of late, she was desiring a break from it. She was getting too damn old to have to worry about her husband or son being killed in the line of hustling or being hauled away to prison to do football numbers. Yogi had to stop and think what life would have been like had she married a regular man. A truck driver, a lawyer, a doctor, or maybe even a military man. That made her think of Merrick, and she snapped out of her daze as she remembered that he was coming by to get her. Yogi quickly freshened up her makeup and ran a comb through her tresses. After she sprayed some perfume, she was satisfied.

Yogi was "that bitch" in her younger days and even now. Her nails stayed done, and she kept a fresh pedicure. Whether she chose to rock her own thick hair in a classy bob-style cut or chose to rock a weave and go for a slightly longer look, she was always put together, down to her always matching bra and panty sets. Married or not, she would never go in the presence of another man, or anyone for that matter, and not be on her A game. She was married, not dead or blind, and anyone with eyes could see that Merrick was a fine-ass man. Yogi never stepped out on Carlton, and she wasn't sure that she ever would. But with all the shit he'd put her through, he just better hope and pray that all she did was think about how fine Merrick was. She had no doubt in her mind that if she applied the smallest amount of pressure, she could have Merrick or any other man she wanted, but she wasn't going to act on it. Just knowing that she still had it was good enough for her. Especially when she was married to a man who acted as if he'd forgotten just how bad she really was.

Chapter Nine

King looked down at the text message from Sloan, and he made a detour. Since she wanted to talk, he was going to her home rather than the office. She would be leaving in a day to do some press and would be gone for three days. With all that was going on out in the streets, King didn't mind Sloan being away. Her growing popularity had people pulling out phones and snapping pictures of her whenever they got a chance, and she'd been spotted out with King one too many times for people to keep thinking they simply had a business relationship. When a man is at war, those closest to him are often attacked in an effort to hurt him, and King didn't need anyone trying to get the bright idea to come at Sloan. Outside her house, King parked his car while wondering what she had to talk to him about.

When she opened the door, it was easy to see that she had been going through it. Sloan looked terrible, and King immediately felt bad for her. Her red, swollen eyes made him step inside the home and eye her with full concern. "Are you good, *mami?* What's wrong?" King's eyes darted around the living room as if he expected the cause of her pain to be something physical that he could see.

"No, I'm not good, King." Sloan's voice was hoarse. "I was up all night stressing this pregnancy. Everything in me is telling me to put everything after the career that I worked so hard for, but the thought of even calling the clinic to make an appointment for an abortion almost makes me physically ill. If I'm this much of a mess at just the thought of ending it, how will I be in the actual room?" Sloan's eyes were full of worry, and King pulled her into his body and hugged her tight.

"Maybe if the decision is this hard for you, that's a pretty good sign that you don't need to do it, Sloan. You will not be the first artist to have a baby, and whatever I have to do to help you and make this a smooth transition for you, then I will. I will be right here by your side every step of the way."

"Will you?" her voice cracked. "Because every day you wake up stressed about this beef shit. Your family can't move without security. Your friend's girlfriend got killed. You've lost friends. When all this is over, I'm supposed to be sure that you'll be left standing?"

"Yes, you are, because I'm telling you I am. I have this under control. You can bet the bank on this, and we can do this. I know we can." King grabbed Sloan's hands and gazed into her eyes.

Sloan just nodded. She was drained mentally and physically and scared out of her mind, but she was tired of being conflicted. There were plenty of reasons to end this pregnancy. But his reassurance and seeing how badly he wanted this baby made her willing to trust him. King kissed Sloan passionately. Sloan was finally able to relax her body in King's arms. It was the first time since she found out about her pregnancy that she was able to do so.

"I'll never let anyone harm you," King spoke into her mouth as he continued the passionate kiss. Deep down inside, he was praying that it was a promise that he'd be able to keep. He would go to the ends of the earth for Sloan and his unborn child, but no one knew if that would even be enough.

King broke the kiss and pulled back so he could pull Sloan's shirt over her head. With a lick of his lips, he cupped her breasts in his hands and admired them. Maybe he was tripping, but her breasts seemed juicier already. In the blink of an eye, King was devouring her body parts with his mouth, and Sloan was moaning with her head back and eyes closed. Pregnancy had her extra sensitive in all of her most sacred parts, and King's mouth felt heavenly on her. King placed a trail of kisses from her breasts up to her chin. Sloan couldn't take any more teasing, and she fumbled anxiously with his belt buckle. Maybe it was hormones, or maybe it was his reassurance, but she had never wanted him so badly in her life.

When she had King's dick in her hand, Sloan dropped to her knees and took him into her mouth hungrily. "Ummmmm," King moaned deeply as he watched the top of Sloan's head.

She made eye contact and gazed into King's eyes as she ran her tongue along the length of his penis before sucking on his balls, then deep throating him. She was showing out, and King was loving every moment of it. Sexing Sloan was way better than arguing with her. Sloan cleaned the saliva from his member and stood up. King was ready to ravish the pussy, and he yanked her leggings down forcefully. When he saw that she wasn't wearing panties, his dick got even harder, if that was possible. Seconds later, he bent Sloan over the couch, and her moans came out choppy.

"King! Right there, baby. Please don't stop," Sloan begged as she caressed her own breasts and pulled her lips into her mouth. Her eyelids began to flutter, and she gripped the couch harder as King stroked her into an intense orgasm. "Yessss, baby," she cried out, coaching him on and stroking his ego. That was a new record for King. He had Sloan coming in less than two minutes. Pregnant pussy was like that for sure.

"Shit, Sloan," King panted as he pumped in and out of her. Her gushiness was putting a vise grip on his dick, and the way she was throwing it back and moaning his name made it all better. He placed kisses along her shoulder, neck, and back after he erupted into her, leaving them both breathing hard.

"You got me wanting to miss work and lie up with you all day." He kissed the back of her neck. "I can already tell where my favorite place is going to be."

Sloan smiled and stood up. "You're going to have to get in where you fit in. Since we're keeping this baby, I want to spend the next eight months or so working my butt off. By the time I enter my ninth month of pregnancy, I want to be able to relax and enjoy waiting on my baby. After that, I want to enjoy motherhood for a few months before I even think of going back in the studio or on the road, so we have to make these next few months count."

Sloan's forehead had a light coat of sweat on it, causing some of her hair to stick to her face, and King gently stroked the hair out of her face. "I'm definitely down for that." He placed a kiss on her lips. King now had a real reason to make as swift an exit from the game as he could.

Addie and Kenny sat on the couch watching one of Sloan's videos on YouTube for what seemed like the hundredth time. Addie couldn't believe that Sloan was on the way to becoming rich and famous. Her mouth was damn near watering for a piece of the action. She wanted in on Sloan's newfound fortune, and she didn't have time to waste. A thought occurred to her, and she looked at Kenny with excitement. "I'll tell her I'm sick and that we've racked up a bunch of debt due to medical bills. I'll tell her I'm about to lose the house. No one with a heart will let their mother be put out on the street."

Kenny simply grunted. He was with the plan, but seeing how excited Addie was made him aware that she may have been slightly delusional to believe that it would be that easy. They weren't Sloan's favorite people, so she just might not give a damn if they were about to be homeless. "Or maybe you could sell some interviews to some of those blogs or something. Give them a little bit of dirt on Sloan."

Addie rolled her eyes and looked at Kenny. "You ever heard the saying that you catch more flies with honey than vinegar? The interviews and blog money will run out. But if Sloan gets rich and we're on her good side, we might reap the benefits over and over. Use your head!" she snapped.

"Whatever you say," he grumbled.

Addie looked at the screen with stars in her eyes. She forgot all about the fact that Sloan hadn't spoken a word to her or visited her in seven years. Addie pushed it to the back of her mind that Sloan hated her guts because she was a poor excuse for a mother. Just like Addie had managed to convince herself that she wasn't a bad mother, she was also managing to convince herself that Sloan would forgive her. Her daughter was the answer to her broke-ass prayers. Addie's brain began working overtime as she tried to think of a way to contact Sloan. "I need her number." She nudged Kenny. "How can we get it?"

"I don't know. Ask your mother." Kenny's eyes were glued to the television screen just as Addie's had been, but his was for a different reason, and Addie snapped out of her trance long enough to call him out on it.

"Why are you staring at her like that?" Addie snapped. "You're damn near salivating at the mouth. You are so disrespectful. You don't even try to hide it when you eye fuck other women. You do it right in my face."

It was in Kenny's nature to deny everything that Addie ever accused him of, but he really didn't want to get on her bad side now. In the event that Sloan did give her mother some money, Kenny needed in on the payday. He couldn't get a decent job, and times were hard as hell. Anything that Addie could get out of Sloan would help them both, and he desperately wanted in on the action. Kenny looked over at his fuming wife and went into acting mode.

"That's my stepdaughter. Watch out with all that bullshit. I told you about that jealous shit. You're my wife, and I only see you. Now, like I said, call your mother. I'm sure she has Sloan's number."

"You know my mother isn't going to give me Sloan's number. The family she did keep in touch with she managed to get to side with her. My mom will talk to me, but she won't talk to me about Sloan, and you know that. I'm going to have to find another way." Just that fast, Addie was able to forget her husband's wandering eye, and it was like that far too often.

When it came to believing anyone and choosing sides, Addie always sided with Kenny, and it cost her a relationship with her only child. For the past seven years, Addie had no idea of what was going on with Sloan, and that was how Sloan preferred it. Addie and her husband were both toxic, and to anyone with good sense, they could tell that Addie was jealous of Sloan. Sloan reminded her of everything that she wasn't. She didn't even care that she hadn't seen her daughter in years. It didn't keep her up at night or make her feel bad, but seeing that Sloan was on her way to stardom was good enough for Addie. It made her want to go all out to reconcile with Sloan. She knew she was going to have to put on the performance of a lifetime for the money, and she was willing to do whatever it took.

Texas licked his lips and gave Donna a sexy smirk. "You get everything you wanted at the mall?"

She matched his lustful gaze and moved from her position on the couch. Donna straddled his lap and instantly felt his manhood start to grow beneath her bottom. "I did. Thank you for looking out." Her voice held a sexy tone, and Texas knew she would be thanking him with some pussy. He hoped it was good, because he blew a bag on her ass. After only a few days of conversation, he decided that she was cool enough for him to apply a little bit of pressure. And what better pressure was there than money?

"You know that ain't nothing to a real nigga. How do you know the chick Imani though?"

Texas didn't miss how Donna's eyes instantly narrowed. He held back a smirk while he waited on her to respond. Donna didn't take him as the disrespectful type, and he had just given her a large amount of money, so she didn't want to fly off the handle and overreact. "We had a few college classes together. I haven't seen her in a while. Not until today in the mall. Why, what's up?"

"Nah, my man tried to get me to tell you to put him down with her, but I just heard something that has me hesitant. Apparently, my nigga Red was her baby daddy, but nobody knew about this. Not even his mother. Red is gone now, so it wouldn't really matter, but still . . ." Texas's voice trailed off.

Donna shook her head. "Your friend Red damn sure got around. I don't know who her baby daddy is though. Like I said, today was my first time seeing her in a minute. The last time I saw Imani, her stomach was flat as hell, and she didn't have any kids. So, that tells you it's been a while."

Texas nodded his head while he tried to figure out how he was going to carry the situation. "Well, find out if she's single. My man Ron is solid," Texas lied. Ron was a pussy hound, but that wasn't his business.

"I don't know." Donna was skeptical. "I try to stay away from the matchmaker thing because if it goes left, I don't want anyone saying it's my fault, but we'll see what happens. We're supposed to link one weekend and go to the club."

"That sounds like a plan to me." Texas placed his hands on the small of Donna's back. She was coming in handy for sure, and for more than just wetting his dick up. "You all comfortable on my lap and shit. You getting my joint hard." Texas didn't want to come off like Donna owed him just because he had given her some money, but if she wasn't trying to fuck, she should climb off his lap with the teasing and shit.

Donna smirked and began grinding on Texas's lap. "I feel it too."

"Okay now. You startin' some shit that I hope you're prepared to finish."

Donna eased off his lap and stood up. She pulled her shirt over her head and stared into Texas's eyes as she reached behind her and unclasped her bra. She had no problem rewarding Texas with a little treat for his generosity. She was curious about his sex game anyway. What she felt while sitting on his lap certainly felt like it could do some damage if he knew how to work it.

Texas maintained eye contact as he unbuckled his jeans, reached inside his boxers, and pulled his dick out. Donna sauntered over and stood in between his legs before squatting down and taking him into her mouth. Texas threw his head back in ecstasy and closed his eyes as Donna performed magic.

Chapter Ten

"Thank you." Yogi gave Merrick a smile as he held the car door open for her. She had to tell him once before that even though he was supposed to be acting as her security, she wasn't going to be riding in the back of the SUV like he was her chauffeur. Yogi preferred to sit in the front of the vehicle beside him.

She needed to pick a few items up from the grocery store for the Sunday dinner that she wanted to prepare. Yogi was old school, and she wasn't going through any of them damn apps like Instacart. She wanted to go get the items herself. Always one to keep it professional, Merrick nodded his head at Yogi and closed the door once she was securely in the vehicle. He walked around to the driver's side of the car, and Yogi stole a few glances at him. Merrick was one fine-ass man. Inside the car, he kept his eyes straight ahead.

"Which store would you like to go to?"

Yogi spoke to him in a friendly and polite tone. "Don't speak to me like you're a robot and I'm just someone you're here to service. You don't have to be so expression-less. If I have to trust you with my life, then you have to at least be someone I'm comfortable with."

Merrick knew that being too friendly and not focused was the easiest way to be sidetracked. He didn't need any distractions. Not when he'd been hired to protect Yogi, Imani, Khristian, and whoever else in the family may need his services at the moment. King was paying him damn good money, and he wasn't about to mess up. In addition to that, a blind man could see that Yogi was a very attractive woman. As well as a very married one. Merrick didn't want to disrespect Yogi, Carlton, or their union, so he kept it very light and professional. Smiling wasn't even something that he did often, but he forced a small one for Yogi.

"I don't sound like a robot. I just want to be professional and respectful."

Yogi acted as if she didn't hear him. She looked over at his hand. "I don't see a wedding band. Are you married?"

Merrick attempted to remain patient with Yogi. He wasn't afraid of a soul, but he was a smart man, and he didn't want problems with Carlton or King for coming off the wrong way toward Yogi. He wasn't sure of a polite way to tell her that was none of her business or not necessary information in order for him to protect her. She didn't have to know a thing about him. Yogi just seemed to be in a talkative mood that day. The aroma of her perfume filled the car, and Merrick kept his eyes on the road. She still hadn't answered his question about what store she wanted to go to, so he was going to go to the nearest one.

"I'm not sure why me being married or not being married matters. Do you always question the help?" He turned toward her and gave her a small smile to let her know that he meant no harm by his question, but he wasn't getting personal with her.

Yogi pouted a bit, and it took some effort for Merrick to keep from smiling and shaking his head. He knew a spoiled woman when he saw one, and Yogi was definitely a very spoiled woman. The men in her life always gave her what she wanted and let her call the shots, and that was what she was used to. Him not answering her question made Yogi stick out her bottom lip, and Merrick had to focus his eyes on the road to keep from thinking about how fine she was sitting beside him in a bright yellow sundress. It was already hard to keep his thoughts pure, and she wasn't making it any easier. Merrick was as tough as they came, and he couldn't believe that he was letting Yogi wear him down.

"I'm not married, Ms. Yogi. You good with that answer?"

"If you didn't want to tell me, you didn't have to." Yogi looked out of the window as her pouting continued. Merrick pulled up at the store and placed the gear in park. Yogi stayed seated until he came around and opened the door for her.

Since she had on heels, Merrick extended his hand toward her, and she grabbed it as she stepped out of the SUV. Merrick accompanied Yogi inside the store, and as she shopped, her attitude seemed to disappear. "We're having Sunday dinner. You should come by."

"Your husband made it clear that inside the house you guys were good. My services are only needed when you're outside the house."

Yogi sucked her teeth and rolled her eyes. "Why do you have to be so difficult? I'm obviously not asking you to come for your services if I'm inviting you to Sunday dinner. I don't know what you're used to, but as I said before, if I have to trust you with my life, I can treat you like family. Since you don't have a wife to cook for you, a little Sunday dinner won't hurt."

Yogi walked off pushing the cart, and Merrick walked behind her, thinking, *this woman is something else.*

King watched Sloan as she got dressed for the day. She had a 5:00 a.m. photo shoot scheduled, then an interview, followed by a studio session. King was watching her closely because she'd spent the entire day before at a video shoot and had only gotten six hours of sleep.

He was worried that she was overdoing it, and he was starting to second-guess his agreement that she would go hard for the next eight months and then sit down. He didn't want her stressed and exhausted. In an effort to make things easier for her, he hired a chef to cook for her, a maid service to clean her home, and he booked weekly massages for her. Sloan would get hair and makeup done at the shoot, so she woke up, showered, and put on some sweats and a tank top.

"Are you sure you're okay?" King asked her as she drank a smoothie. "Do I need to start making your appointments later in the day so you can get more rest?"

Sloan smiled at King. "I'm fine, really. That IV drip that I got on set last night really helped. It just reminded me that as long as I eat healthy and stay hydrated, the fatigue won't be too bad. I won't lie, though, I plan to be done in the studio by five p.m., and I'm coming home and getting right in bed. You don't even have to worry about that."

King walked over to Sloan and wrapped his arms around her. He had done his research, and he found a company that did various kinds of IV drips on patients. You could get them for hangovers, being dehydrated, et cetera. When he found out it was safe for pregnant women, he arranged for her to get an IV the day before while she was on break in between shooting. He also made sure that her driver always had ice-cold bottled water and Gatorade in the car for her at all times. He didn't want Sloan to regret agreeing to have this child at the same time that she was trying to get her career off the ground. If King had to choose, he would choose his child every time, but he wasn't in Sloan's position. It scared him to think that Sloan might wake up one day regretting her decision to keep the baby.

"I just want you to be comfortable and not stressed. Whatever I have to do to make your life easier, let me know. With the videos and photo shoots, you can be a success with minimal traveling. I don't want to push you."

"King, I'm fine. I take power naps in the car, and most times, I'm sitting down. I spent a lot of time on set yesterday sitting. I sat to get hair and makeup done. I sat while they shot scenes that I wasn't in. I even got a small nap during lunch break. I'm okay, baby."

Satisfied with her answer, King placed a kiss on her lips. Sloan got a text message that the driver was outside, so she grabbed her smoothie and her bag, and King walked her out to the car. After he kissed her goodbye, he headed back inside the house to get ready for his day.

King had a long day ahead of him as well, and he appreciated that Jenna was able to meet with him so early. After a morning run, he ate some breakfast, took a shower, and got dressed to meet her at a coffee shop. Jenna was an event planner, and King had plans to throw a party for Sloan in the next two weeks. Her birthday was coming up, and King was going to throw her a party that would make everyone else's party look childish. Two weeks wasn't a lot of time when it came to putting together an event of that magnitude, and that was why he was going to hire the best. King wasn't going to spare any expense in the effort to make sure Sloan had a birthday that she would never forget.

He knew fate was on his side because things were lining up perfectly for him. Things with Sloan and King moved rather quickly, and even though they had some long conversations, he didn't know a lot about her family. And that was information that King was going to need if he was going to be able to give Sloan the surprise of a lifetime at the party that he was planning for her.

Now all he had to do was handle this shit he had going on with Chin and Red's people so he could finally move without looking over his shoulder every few seconds. King had a baby on the way, and becoming a legit business and family man was sounding more and more appealing to him.

Chapter Eleven

Imani smiled at her son and made faces and noises at him as she unbuckled and picked him up out of his car seat. The great thing about her moving out of Yogi and Carlton's house was that they missed Caleb terribly, and Yogi was always calling and asking to babysit him. This was the perfect day for Yogi to watch Caleb because it was the night that Imani wanted to go out with Donna, and Yogi had agreed to keep the baby overnight. Imani was so excited to be going out. She loved being a mother, but being cooped up in the house washing bottles, doing laundry, and having a baby attached to her hip at all times was becoming a bit draining. Imani needed a social life, and she was going to have to figure out how to balance motherhood with still being young and wanting to have her own life.

Imani flung Caleb's bag over her shoulder and walked up to the front door. Before she could even ring the bell, Yogi was opening the door with a wide smile on her face, reaching for the baby.

"Oh, how I've missed him." She held Caleb in front of her face and rubbed his nose with hers. The scene made Imani smile, but it also made her stomach feel queasy. The way that Yogi loved Caleb was amazing, and if she knew who Caleb really was, it would kill her.

"Imani," Carlton's voice boomed as she stepped into the front room. She almost wished that she had stopped by when he wasn't home.

"A detective came by looking for you today. He said he needed to talk to you about some new developments in the case. I didn't know your new address offhand, so I just told him that you weren't living here anymore. You might want to reach out to him though." The look that Carlton was giving her was a stern one, and she could read between the lines. He was tired of detectives showing up at his home.

Imani was tired of the questions herself. "Look, I told them everything I know. I'm not sure what more they want from me." Imani had no intention of calling the detectives.

Yogi sat down on the couch and put Caleb in her lap.

"If he said he had a new development, maybe he wants to share something with you. I think you should find out what it is ASAP. Maybe he found out who put the bomb underneath your car, and King and Kareem can get some relief."

"Did he leave a card?" Imani asked in a fake chipper voice. She was tired of the entire fiasco with the police. She knew exactly who put the bomb underneath her car, and King and Kareem would never get closure. Even if they killed Carlton for it, it would unleash too many other skeletons, and things would never be the same. King and Kareem would kill Carlton, and Yogi just might kill her.

Every time Imani thought about how out of control things got with her and Carlton, a chill ran up her spine. Images of falling down a flight of stairs while she was pregnant and damn near being charred alive in her car made her feel like things could get out of control again and her life could be at stake. Carlton passed Imani the card, and she put it in her pocket.

"I'm going to get going. Thanks for letting him stay. He just ate an hour ago. He has plenty of milk and baby food in his bag. I'll come to get him tomorrow around noon."

Yogi grabbed Caleb's hand and waved at Imani with it. "Tell Mommy goodbye."

Imani leaned down and kissed Caleb on the cheeks. "Bye, fat man. I'll see you tomorrow."

Imani slipped from the house and thought about all that she had to do before she met Donna. She needed to get her lashes done, she needed to get her nails done, and she needed to buy some razors so she could shave her legs. Imani had a full day ahead, and she hoped it would lead to an eventful night. Imani's ringing phone made her turn the volume on her radio down and grab her phone from her lap. Imani groaned when she saw that Carlton was calling.

"Hello?" She kept her tone emotionless and even.

"You need to handle that shit with the police and handle it now." Carlton's tone was low and ice cold. It was almost threatening, and that chill crept up on Imani again. She was even more tired of dealing with Carlton than she was of dealing with the police. It would hurt Yogi, but if Imani got the money, she would take her son and leave town just to get away from Carlton's sadistic ass.

"I thought you told them that Caleb belonged to Red."

"I did. What else do you want me to do? I moved out of your house. I can't help that they're still coming there. Maybe if you hadn't tried to murder me, Tiana wouldn't be dead, and we wouldn't be going through this," Imani stated boldly. She could tell by the brief silence that the words she just spoke infuriated Carlton, but she couldn't take them back.

"If you ever say that shit again, I'll cut your lips off your fucking face, bitch. If you would've listened to me in the first place, we wouldn't be going through any of this shit. You wanted it and you got it. Now, fix it."

He ended the call, and it took everything in Imani not to scream. She hated that man's guts. Imani tossed her phone in the passenger seat. She was determined to go out and have a good time regardless of whether she met someone, but it would be epic for her to meet someone who could save her ass. She didn't even want to need Carlton's help paying her rent. Imani needed to get it together and fast. She didn't have the nerve to strip, so that was out of the question for sure.

Imani did everything that she needed to do, and then she went home and showered before she started pregaming. Cognac was her vice of choice tonight, and it always put her in the mood to get on her Lil' Kim shit. Lil' Kim may have been before her time, but Imani's mother was the original hot girl. Imani learned everything she knew about milking niggas from her mother, and Lil' Kim's music was often the anthems that Imani heard playing throughout their home when she was a young girl.

The plan was to meet at the club, and by the time Imani met up with Donna in the parking lot, she was buzzed and feeling good.

"Heyyyy, boooo," she sang as she hugged Donna and did the customary air kisses. Both women were looking good and feeling better, and all Imani wanted to do was have a good time and maybe find a new dick to sit on. Her sex life had been nonexistent since ending things with Carlton, or since he ended things with her when she wouldn't abort Caleb.

"Who just had a baby not too long ago?" Donna asked as she looked Imani up and down. "You look the fuck good!"

"Thank you," Imani gushed. She had been through the phase of feeling insecure about her body, but Donna's compliment along with the alcohol had her on cloud nine.

The women entered the club and headed straight for the bar. The DJ was playing all the hottest songs, and Imani was lit. She was twerking on Donna and having a grand ole time. She had been in the club for an hour and downed another drink when she saw him. Kareem was standing off to the side with a drink in his hand, and Imani felt all hot and bothered. The plan was to still try to wriggle her way into Kareem's life. Imani eyed him and how he was standing there looking all gangsta and shit. Imani bit her bottom lip as she contemplated going over to him. The liquor in her system had her feeling bold as hell, but Imani didn't want to come on too strong. She was sure that he was still mourning, and she didn't want to come across as disrespectful, especially since, according to Tiana's mother, Imani was the reason that she was dead.

As if he felt Imani's eyes burning a hole into him, Kareem looked over and locked eyes with Imani. He chucked his chin up in a form of greeting, and Imani gave him a smile and a small wave.

"My friend Texas has a friend named Ron who was asking about you. He saw you in the mall the day that we ran into each other," Donna informed her, causing Imani to tear her eyes away from Kareem.

Ron sounded like a plan B in case things didn't pop off like she wanted them to with Kareem. "For real? Is he cute?" Imani directed her attention to Donna.

"He doesn't look better than my baby, but he's not hard on the eyes at all. I tried to do a little discreet digging, and I think his pockets are heavy enough."

Imani grinned like the Cheshire cat. "That's all I needed to hear. Put me in the game, coach."

"You got a baby by Red?" Peaches appeared in Imani's face out of nowhere and was looking like she wanted war with the girl.

It was still fresh in her mind the ass whooping that Donna handed her, but Peaches refused to be punked in the club. It was well known that this bitch, Imani, was going around saying she had a baby by Red, and Peaches needed her to stand on that. Peaches didn't give a damn if he was dead. Donna was one in a million who could whoop her, but she refused to believe that she'd get her ass whooped twice. There was no way she was letting this shit with Imani slide.

Imani's mouth went dry as she eyed the angry woman standing in front of her. Obviously, her telling the detective that Red was her baby daddy had gotten out, and Imani wasn't prepared for that, but she had to save face.

"Who the fuck are you?" Imani frowned her face up and pretended not to know who Peaches was.

"I'm Red's girlfriend, and I don't appreciate you lying on the dead, bitch!"

Imani ran her tongue across her teeth and shook her head. "If Red isn't here to deny my child, then you can't say shit. You may have been Red's girl, but his dick wasn't exclusive to you, and you know that shit. Now, let him rest. The detective asked me a question, and I answered. If I was pressed about money or anything, I'd be running in behind Red's friends and family begging like you're known to do."

Peaches was so mad that her face turned red. She was ready to beat Imani's ass when Kareem stepped in between them. "Do we have a problem?"

Peaches knew that Kareem was her man's enemy, but Red was no more, and she still had to live. Kareem was fine, and he had paper, so she wasn't trying to get on his bad side. "I'll catch you later, bitch," Peaches threatened Imani before walking off.

Kareem watched Peaches walk away, and then he turned to face Imani. If she was beefing with Peaches, maybe Caleb did belong to Red, but the shit didn't make sense to Kareem. A lot of shit wasn't making sense, and that wasn't sitting well with him. Somebody had some funny shit going on, and he was ready to get to the bottom of it. Until he did, he felt like he was failing Tiana.

"You good?" He eyed Imani in her tight dress.

Tiana hadn't been dead for too long, but Kareem was a man, and maybe coming out to the club had been the wrong thing to do. Every time he saw a fine-ass woman in a skimpy outfit, his dick would stiffen. He thought about the fact that, at some point, he'd have to deal with the opposite sex if only for the reason of getting his dick wet. He had jacked his dick so much in prison that Kareem had no desire to do that shit while he was out in the world. Sticking dick into a female didn't mean that he didn't love Tiana, and she wasn't coming back. If he had a choice, she'd be right there by his side, but the choice had been taken from him.

"Yeah, I'm good." Imani bit her bottom lip sexily. With the alcohol in her system, Kareem was looking even better than he usually did. He smelled good, he was dressed nice, and it was taking everything in her not to start twerking on him when one of her favorite songs came on. "How are the kids doing? How is Keana?"

"She's doing good. She has her days as far as missing her mother. All the kids do, but she's good. When you had to pick her up for me, she had a stomach bug. My baby was out of it for two days, then she was back like cooked crack."

Imani smiled. "That's good. I'm glad, and don't forget that my offer still stands. Anytime that I'm free I will babysit for you."

"I'll keep that in mind. You be safe tonight." Kareem walked off, and Imani found herself wishing that he would have at least flirted with her a little, but she reminded herself that the man was grieving. Her disappointment soon faded when two fine-ass men came up to her and Donna.

Imani could tell right away which one was Donna's boo by the way he was eyeing her. Donna smiled and blushed and then looked over at Imani. "This is my boo, Texas, and this is his friend, Ron. Guys, this is Imani."

Ron was fucking Imani with his eyes, and he was turning her on. It had been a long time since she'd been intimate with a man. These days, her nights were spent cuddling with Caleb. Imani was yearning for a long, thick dick to apply some pressure to her. "How you doing, Miss Imani? You single?"

"I am. What about you? I know how men are, and I'm not interested in being a side chick." She was very forward. Imani had enough sneaking around and getting caught up with Carlton, and she was over that shit. She needed a man of her own.

"I'm single as a dollar bill, baby. What you drinking?" Ron couldn't stop looking Imani up and down. She was fine as hell, and he wanted to bed that by the end of the night. He'd also peeped her talking to Kareem, and that was even better. If she was cool with that nigga like that, maybe she could lead him to Kareem and King. Only time would tell, but Ron would never be mad at the possibility of killing two birds with one stone.

Ron bought Imani a drink and stayed glued to her side for the rest of the night. When they left the club, Imani had nothing against hooking up with Ron, but she wasn't thirsty enough or desperate enough to let him come to her place, especially since Carlton's demonic ass was paying the rent. She suggested that he get a hotel room, and Ron obliged. As she followed him to the hotel, all Imani could do was hope that her first ride back in the rodeo was a good one. If she was linking with this nigga and his dick was garbage, she'd be mad as hell.

Chapter Twelve

King glanced over at Sloan and smiled at the fact that she was asleep in the back of the car they were riding in. Her birthday was in twenty-four hours, and she had to catch a flight at 6:00 a.m., so King was taking her to the surprise that he had for her.

Sloan had a light day in the studio, but then she had to get her hair, nails, and makeup done. The baby she was carrying was tiring her ass out, but Sloan was being a real trooper, and King appreciated that. Her first single with a feature from a popular artist was officially dropping on her birthday along with the music video that she had shot.

Earlier, she posted some of the pictures from the photo shoot that she'd done, and they were so dope that King couldn't stop staring at them. Ten minutes after she posted the first picture, it had over 15,000 likes on Instagram, and just like that, she was going to be able to get monthly checks from IG. With 534,000 followers, Sloan could go live, post pictures and videos, and monetize her account. Another source of income was secured for her, and she was grateful. Every time Sloan started to think about how tired she was, or how she felt sick, or all she wanted to do was rest, she thought about how far she'd come, and she'd get a burst of energy.

When the driver pulled up at the venue, King reached over and rubbed Sloan's arm. The car ride had only lasted for sixteen minutes, but in that amount of time she'd fallen into a deep sleep, and that let King know just how tired she was. He rubbed harder. "Sloan, we're here, baby."

Since it was a special occasion, she was dressed in a gold sequined gown with gold heels, and her makeup was done to perfection. Sloan's naturally long hair was styled in loose curls, and she looked amazing. When she traveled and performed, wearing her real hair wasn't an option for many reasons, so for this occasion, Sloan just wanted to give herself a break from weaves and wigs. She opened her eyes and looked around. Embarrassed, she wiped a tiny bit of drool from her mouth. Sloan could fall asleep anywhere. She never felt anything like it before, but the short naps that she took often saved her life because the growing child inside her was taking all of her energy. It was like there was a vampire sucking the life out of her. But it was something that most pregnant women went through, and Sloan could only hope that it would pass.

"I'm sorry," she apologized to King.

He pulled her close to him. "You don't have to apologize to me. I know why you're tired. I could watch you sleep all day." He planted a kiss on her cheek as the car came to a stop, and the driver got out and walked to the rear of the car so he could open the door for the couple. King got out of the car first, and then he held his hand out for Sloan. The security he had trailing the SUV he was in got out of the car they were in and positioned themselves in front of King and Sloan and behind them. King had rented out the entire venue, so the only people inside were by invitation only.

"What is this?" Sloan asked as King gripped her hand. She sensed it was something bigger than dinner.

King didn't miss a beat. He continued looking straight ahead as he held her hand and led the way into the building. "It's your birthday dinner," was his reply.

Twenty seconds later, Sloan gasped as she was led into a large room filled with people. Sloan didn't have a lot of friends and family she was close with. She had two best friends she spoke to weekly, and she was pretty close with three of her cousins and an uncle. Yet, the room was filled with more than sixty people. Some of them were from the music industry, and Sloan's friends and some of her family were present. Her eyes misted with tears, and she looked over at King. This was truly unexpected, especially since she hadn't introduced King to anyone in her family. "You did all this for me?" She didn't want to cry and mess up her makeup, but the sentiment of the moment had the tears threatening to fall. People started coming up to Sloan, greeting her and hugging her, and she was overwhelmed. It had to be pregnancy hormones because Sloan learned long ago that crying didn't solve anything, so she stopped doing it. She couldn't stop the tears from falling, however, and King looked on with pride.

He was glad that he could do something to surprise Sloan and put a smile on her face. She was carrying his child, and whether she knew it or not, from the moment he found out, she became a permanent fixture in his life he would die for. When Sloan's eyes landed on a table in the corner of the room and she saw all of the gifts, she placed her head on King's chest and allowed herself to cry while silently thanking God that her makeup was waterproof. King wrapped his arms around her and let Sloan be overcome with emotion. When she was done crying, she stepped back slightly and wiped her tears.

"You really didn't have to do all of this, but thank you, King. This is really the best birthday that I've ever had."

King used his finger to lovingly swipe one of her tears away. "Anything for you, and I mean that from the bottom of my heart. You deserve the best of everything from this day forward. Anything I can do to put a smile on your face, I will. I hope you know that."

The way he gazed into her eyes, Sloan knew that he was sincere. She knew she made the right choice by agreeing to have his baby. He was right. This wasn't fifteen years ago. Women could have careers and babies, so if her music career didn't take off, then it simply wasn't meant to be, and she would be okay with that.

A waiter stopped at Sloan's side, and she politely declined a glass of champagne off the tray that he was carrying, but King grabbed one. Sloan eyed the decorations and the way that everyone was dressed up, and she couldn't stop smiling. When one of her songs began to play, she really got into the spirit, and she began to dance on King. For the first thirty minutes, Sloan had the time of her life. She danced, she laughed and joked, and she tasted some of the best food.

Sloan was finally tired of standing and was about to take a seat when the air was snatched from her lungs. She had to do a double take at who she saw walking through the door. For a moment, she even stopped breathing. Her head whipped in King's direction, and he looked pleased. He didn't have a clue, and Sloan hated that she had to use this day to be the one to fill him in. He instantly peeped the look on her face and knew that something was wrong. He looked from her to Kenny and Addie, then back to Sloan. She looked like she was about to pass out.

"Baby, what's wrong? Are you okay?"

Before she could answer him, her mother and her stepfather were up on her. "Happy early birthday, baby. I'm so happy that King invited us." Addie had the nerve to be smiling like she was truly happy to see her daughter, but Sloan knew better.

"Please have security escort them out," she spoke in a low voice to King while never taking her eyes off the woman in front of her.

King frowned up his face a bit. This shit was going left real fast. Had he known that Sloan didn't fuck with her mother like that, he would have never invited them. Seeing how pissed Sloan looked made him realize that he'd messed up. King could practically feel the heat radiating off her body. He signaled security over, and Addie started to panic.

"Sloan, don't be like that. I haven't seen you in years. Why can't you let bygones be bygones? Whatever grudge you have against us, you need to let that go," she pleaded as security took long strides to get to King. "I'm sick, Sloan. I need money for medical bills. You're really going to leave your mother out in the cold?"

Sloan couldn't take it anymore. Even after all they'd put her through, here they were yet again ruining her moment and begging. Sloan was on her way to stardom, but she wasn't rich yet. Her checking account only held the money that it did because when she signed with King's label, he gave her a generous advance. She had no idea when the money from her music would start rolling in, and she didn't like asking King for money. So, she had to wait. But even when she did reach the financial status that people already assumed she had, she wasn't giving her bitch-ass mother a dime. Sloan was infuriated that they even had the gall to show up and ask her for anything. She turned to walk away, and her mother's voice penetrated her ears.

"You are such an ungrateful little bitch! I'm your fucking mother. I'm dying and you don't care all over some dumb-ass delusions. You are a delusional person, and you love playing the victim. I can't believe that you really don't care if I die." Addie's voice began to fade as Sloan reached the bathroom.

She snatched the door open with tears in her eyes, and just like that her night was ruined. Sloan grabbed some paper towels and dabbed at her face. She would have rather come face-to-face with Satan than the two ghosts from her past. Sloan had never laid eyes on her child. It wasn't even a child. It was merely an embryo, and even though she thought about abortion, Sloan knew without a shadow of a doubt that she'd die trying to protect her child. Her mother wasn't a mother at all, and it sickened Sloan that women who didn't deserve to have kids often had them with ease while others couldn't get pregnant to save their lives and they so desperately wanted kids.

Sloan was trying to keep the tears at bay and salvage her makeup when the bathroom door opened. Her eyes shifted down, and she was prepared to ignore whoever came into the bathroom until she heard that voice.

"Sloan. Talk to me."

She closed her eyes and exhaled a small breath. She didn't feel like explaining, but he deserved to know the truth. After a few moments of trying to compose herself, she turned to face him. "I don't fuck with my mother or her husband under any circumstances. I know that you didn't know, but, King, I can't ever see them again. I don't want to." Her bottom lip quivered, and he rushed over to her.

"Baby, tell me what's wrong." He moved the hair out of her face. King remained patient while Sloan looked down. He only allowed her to look down for so long before he used his hand to gently lift her head so that he was looking into her eyes.

"My stepfather used to touch me inappropriately." She recalled the painful memory. "When I told my mother, she called me a liar. I was thirteen years old, and she called me everything but a child of God and said I was trying to ruin her life. I tried to kill myself, and when I was in the hospital, I opened up to one of the therapists. They did an investigation, and he was arrested. At his trial, he was found guilty and sentenced to five years in prison. I don't know what's worse: the fact that he only got five years or the fact that she stayed with him," Sloan cried. "My own mother. She chose him over me."

King's body tensed up. He was shaking so hard in anger, and Sloan felt it. She stopped crying long enough to lift her head and look up at him. She had never seen King look so mad before, and it scared her. When he turned his body, she grabbed him. Sloan felt her party had already been ruined, but it would certainly be the talk of the evening if King went back out there and beat Kenny's ass. He deserved it. In Sloan's opinion, no one deserved an ass whooping more than Kenny, but not here and not now. She had a lot to process, but in that moment all she cared about was protecting King.

"It's okay, King. I promise you. Don't do it."

King stared into Sloan's face, trying to calm himself down, but he wanted blood, and he wanted it bad. Sloan grabbed his hands and squeezed them. She was the one who had gone through the traumatic experience, and she was trying to comfort him. "Security had better done their job and gotten that muhfucka out of here because if I see his face, I will end up smiling in a mug shot tonight, and I can promise you that. I can get that's not something you want to talk about, but, baby, had I known, I would've never invited them when they reached out to me. I'm so fucking sorry, Sloan."

"How did they even get in contact with you?"

"Your mom called the studio one day right before you got there, and I felt it was perfect timing because I had just gotten the idea to plan this party for you. I knew you were only able to celebrate today because your schedule is so full, and I wanted you to have a great birthday. I never would have imagined that you weren't talking about your mother because something like this happened to you."

Even through her pain, Sloan found the strength to smile. "This was the best birthday I have ever had, and I won't let them take that from me. They have taken enough from me. The fact that she had the nerve to look in my face and ask me for money pisses me off, but I can't give them my joy. Not on this day. So, thank you so much for this party, and let's go back out there and try to enjoy the rest of it. I'm starving."

King placed a kiss on Sloan's lips and let it linger. Despite her speech, he knew she was still hurting, and he still felt like shit. The one thing King regretted was that he didn't have an address, because if he knew how to find them, then Kenny would be dead before the sun came up. But all in due time. He had just added one more body to his hit list. Possibly two if Addy wanted to go with Kenny.

Chapter Thirteen

Imani walked out of the locker room of the YMCA and ran right into Derrick. She hadn't gone swimming in a few days, and she thought about that when she woke up and her back was killing her. Imani didn't want to take pain medication because it would make her sleepy, and after Yogi had Caleb all weekend, she didn't want to ask her to babysit yet again. Caleb still took quite a few naps during the day, but he was getting to the age where he stayed awake longer, and Imani couldn't take care of him while she was doped up on pain meds. She let Caleb go to the day care inside the YMCA while she swam a few laps. Imani had a lot going on, and she hadn't talked to or seen Derrick since the day he helped her. He was a nice guy, but at this time, Imani just didn't see him fitting into her life. They were from two entirely different worlds.

"Hi." She smiled at him while feeling a little awkward. "How have you been?"

"I've been good. Busy with work and stuff, but I've thought about you."

While Imani hadn't reached out to him, he hadn't reached out to her either, so she wasn't sure why she felt so guilty. Maybe she wasn't his type, and she couldn't even be mad at that. "No offense, but had I been on your mind like that, you would've reached out and asked me out before running into me. It's fine though, Derrick. I'm busy with my son, and you're busy with work. I'll see you around." She shot him another smile before walking off, and at that very moment, she got a text message from Ron.

That made Imani blush. He hadn't disappointed her at all. That dick was some of the best she'd ever had, and Imani was delighted that he had been keeping in touch with her since that night. She wanted some more of that dick ASAP. Imani texted him back as she walked to get Caleb, and she hoped he wanted to link again soon. Maybe she could get Khristian to watch Caleb while she dipped out for a sneaky link. Khristian had come home from college for Sloan's birthday party. Imani still wasn't ready to let Ron know where she lived. Not just yet. For as many times as Carlton tried to kill her and acted like he couldn't stand her, he shouldn't have a problem with her having company, but one could never tell with Carlton. He was unpredictable to say the least, and Imani was done playing with him. He had already promised that the next time he tried to take her life he wouldn't fail.

Imani got Caleb buckled into his car seat. After she snapped her seat belt on, she saw that Kareem was texting her, asking her to babysit. Now that Ron was in the picture, Imani wasn't sure she needed to keep volunteering to be a babysitter for Kareem, but she quickly determined that it was a good idea. *These niggas can switch up at any moment.* Carlton taught her that. So having a plan B would be a good thing. She texted Kareem back and agreed to babysit the kids. She stopped and got food, then went straight to his house.

By the time she reached Kareem's house, it was time for Caleb to eat, so she rang the bell and bounced him, hoping that his crying didn't get louder. Kareem opened the door with the phone to his ear. Imani nodded her head at him and rushed over to the couch so she could feed Caleb. Kareem walked out of the room, and a few minutes later when he walked back in, KJ was behind him, and he was no longer on the phone.

"Your grandma is at the doctor, and I have to make a quick run. Ms. Imani is going to watch you for about an hour." Kareem looked over at her. "Their older cousin will come by to relieve you in an hour."

"Okay." She smiled, then noticed that KJ was glaring at her.

"Why does she have to watch us? Grandma said that she's the reason our mom is dead. She should be dead and not my ma, and then Ma could be here with us." KJ had a frown on his face, and he was glaring at Imani like he hated her guts.

Her body burned with shame and embarrassment. Imani stood up while still holding the bottle in Caleb's mouth. "You know I don't mind helping you, but I'm a little tired of being disrespected every time I come to your home." Imani looked from Kareem to KJ. "I'm very sorry that your mother died, but the person who put a bomb underneath my car is the reason that your mother is no longer here." She snatched Caleb's bag up and headed for the door while Kareem stood in shock.

"What in the fuck is wrong with you?" he chastised his son. "Since when are you bold enough to stand in my face and disrespect adults?"

"But Grandma said—"

"I don't care what your grandma said. What you just said was fucked up and out of pocket. Go to your room and unplug your game systems and bring me your phone." Kareem was two seconds off KJ's ass as he stomped away, but he rushed out of the house to make sure Imani was okay.

Kareem was very angry about Tiana's death, but he wasn't going to blame Imani. He knew all too well that most times innocent people were casualties of war. There had been many times his gunplay affected someone it wasn't meant for. Imani wasn't to blame for someone trying to kill her and getting Tiana instead.

"Imani, I hate that the last few times you came over here trying to help me you were disrespected. That's not fair to you. I checked Tiana's mother about that shit, and I'm going to check KJ."

Imani was so mad that she wouldn't even look Kareem in the eyes. "It's fine."

The way her face was frowned up, Kareem knew that was a lie. She was furious, and she was trying to keep her cool. There wasn't much he could say. He knew the words had to be hurtful. With the way he had to run the streets some days, the more people he had to help him with the kids the better, but it seemed that Imani's help was being sabotaged. He didn't know what else to say, so he just let Imani get in her car and drive off. Then, he headed inside to deal with KJ.

"Hey, big boy! That's a big boy!" Yogi enjoyed the laughter that erupted from Caleb's body every time she tickled him. It had been almost a week since he spent the weekend with her, and Yogi had missed him terribly. She had to admit that even she was shocked at the attachment she had to the baby. If she was like this with him, how would she be with her own grandkids?

The doorbell rang, and Yogi picked Caleb up off the couch and went to answer the door.

"King! Hey, baby." Yogi gave her son air kisses after he stepped into the house.

"How is everything going?" King eyed Caleb and grabbed his hand. "Hey, li'l man." He studied the child, then let out a small chuckle. "That baby been hanging over here so much his ass is starting to look like Carlton."

Yogi laughed and hit him playfully. "Boy, hush."

"He sure doesn't look like Red," King mumbled and studied the child intensely.

"Boy, what are you talking about?" Yogi put Caleb in his walker and sat down on the couch.

"There's something up with this Imani situation, and I just can't figure it out. I don't think she knows who this child's father is, and me and Kareem would love to know. We're in the middle of some real shit, but Imani isn't tied to our family like that. If niggas were trying to get to me or Kareem, why not put a bomb under your car or Tiana's car? The bomb was placed under Imani's car, which means she was the target. Who does she have beef with? Has anyone ever seen this nigga she claimed was Caleb's father at first? When the police questioned her, she put it on a nigga named Red, but no one knows if that's true." King looked truly puzzled.

Yogi sat stumped. She recalled Imani telling them that her child's father didn't want him because he was older than her and married. Now, she was saying it was one of King's peers? Yes, King was older than her, but not the older that Imani implied this man was. Maybe she really didn't know who her child's father was and she was embarrassed.

"I have to tell you something." King broke Yogi from her thoughts, and she gave her undivided attention to her son.

"What is it, dear?"

"We were going to keep it to ourselves just a little while longer, but Sloan is pregnant."

Yogi gasped. "King, that's wonderful news! What do you mean you were going to keep it to yourselves for a bit longer? I'm your mother."

"I know, but we're just superstitious, I guess. Maybe more so me than her. Sloan has a doctor's appointment tomorrow. She's not even here right now. Her flight lands at midnight. This is the beginning of her career, and she's doing a lot of working and traveling. I'm just trying to be cautious."

"She will be okay. Us women were made to carry babies. I'm not saying that rest isn't important, and she surely doesn't need to stress, but working while pregnant isn't a crime. Every woman doesn't have the luxury of being able to sit around for nine months. I've seen women work up until the day they gave birth. She sings. It's not like she's out in a field picking cotton for ten hours a day. Sloan will be just fine."

King chuckled. Only his mother would break it down like that. "You're right, Ma. I guess I was worrying for nothing. I'm still on this thing with Chin though, so for now, Merrick stays around. How is everything going? Are you and Carlton good?"

Yogi rolled her eyes. "I'm always going to be good, and Carlton is Carlton. He's never home and blames work as an excuse. That man could have retired years ago, and if I had to guess, I'd say he wants to. But then he wouldn't be able to use work as an excuse to stay out all day and half the night." Yogi had a look on her face as if she was disgusted by just the thought of her husband.

"Carlton has been Carlton for years," King pointed out.

"That is so. You aren't telling me anything that I don't know, but I don't have to keep putting up with it. Don't be surprised if you come around one day and I'm telling you that I filed for divorce."

King sighed. He had enough going on, and he didn't need to add drama with her and Carlton to the mix. Carlton had already been calling him three to four times a day complaining about his money losses. King knew they would be okay. Carlton and Yogi had been going through the same song and dance for years.

After he spoke to his mother for a little longer, King left, and Yogi looked at a babbling Caleb and smiled. When the baby smiled back, Yogi's blood suddenly ran cold.

"That baby been hanging over here so much his ass is starting to look like Carlton."

King's words played in her mind like a broken record repeating itself. How had she not seen it before? The older Caleb got, he looked nothing like Imani and everything like someone else. Carlton's face was one that she woke up to every day, so when staring at Caleb, it wasn't hard to realize that he had a lot of Carlton's features. They had the same nose, the same eyes.

"He's married, isn't he?"

Yogi remembered asking Imani about Caleb's father when she announced her pregnancy. And he was older. Yogi felt lightheaded. There was no way on God's green earth that Imani and Carlton would play with her like that. She was paranoid. That was it. That had to be it. Yogi was paranoid and tripping.

"There's something up with this Imani situation, and I just can't figure it out. I don't think she knows who this child's father is, and me and Kareem would love to know. We're in the middle of some real shit, but Imani isn't tied to our family like that. If niggas were trying to get to me or Kareem, why not put a bomb under your car or Tiana's car? The bomb was placed under Imani's car, which means she was the target. Who does she have beef with? Has anyone ever seen this nigga she claimed was Caleb's father at first? When the police questioned her, she put it on a nigga named Red, but no one knows if that's true."

Everything about the conversation she just had with her son was bringing more revelations to the forefront, and Yogi felt like she was going to be sick. The more she stared at Caleb, the more she saw her husband. Yogi desperately wanted her mind to be playing tricks on her. She knew Carlton wasn't shit, but this was one time that she wanted to be so wrong about him that she could laugh about it later. The bomb under her car. That was some shit that Carlton would do for sure to one of his enemies. Imani got pushed down some steps. Carlton didn't want the baby, and he tried to kill her. But he loved when Caleb was around. Yogi was so conflicted that it was giving her a headache. She knew what she had to do, and she wasn't waiting on Merrick either. This was one time she would have to defy her son's wishes, but Yogi was a grown woman. She didn't need permission to leave her home.

"Come on, baby." She walked over to Caleb, and just that fast, she felt different. She had been playing the god-mother role to this baby who may have been a product of Carlton's cheating. If Imani and Carlton had dared play with her like that, Yogi was going to kill them both and not think twice about it. This shit was the ultimate disrespect.

Yogi walked out to her car as fast as she could with Caleb in her arms. She buckled him into the car seat that she kept in her car for him.

When Yogi got in the driver's seat, tears filled her eyes. She didn't even know why she was so emotional when she didn't know anything for sure.

Chapter Fourteen

"We have an annual review coming up for our life insurance policy, and I need you to be here in the morning to get your blood drawn," Yogi stated as she sorted through pieces of mail.

Carlton looked at her with a confused expression on his face. "Annual? We've had that policy for the past few years. I've only gotten my blood drawn once in the beginning."

Yogi didn't bat an eye. "It might not be annual, but it's time for them to check our health. We're already locked in, so no matter what they find, the policy won't decrease. However, if they find us to be in good health, we may be eligible for an increase at the same rate."

"Increase? If I die, you already get two million dollars. Damn, that isn't enough? Although in a minute, if your son and his friend don't stop this fucking war, I might be worth more dead than alive." Carlton chuckled while Yogi continued to pretend to be interested in the mail.

"Are you going to cooperate or not?" The way she felt, it would make her feel better to kill his ass and become $2 million richer, but she wasn't there yet. Yogi just needed Carlton to believe what she was saying and not decide to find the policy, call them, and ask questions. Or she'd be screwed.

Yogi had already gone to the store and gotten an at-home DNA testing kit and swabbed Caleb's mouth. She had to be a little bit more creative when it came to getting

Carlton's blood, so thank God Yogi had plenty of money and a few connections. She was actually good friends with a woman whose daughter worked at LabCorp. Her friend's daughter was all too happy to accept the $600 that Yogi offered her to come to her home and draw Carlton's blood. She would pretend to be a contract worker for their insurance company. She was just a phlebotomist, so that way if Carlton asked any questions about the policy, she could just say she didn't have access to that information. Carlton was a smart man, so Yogi had to be calculated when it came to trying to deceive him.

"Yes. What time are they coming, dear?" Carlton decided to try to appease Yogi. She had been acting more and more distant lately, and now that he was completely done with Imani, he missed the connection and the bond that he used to have with his wife. Carlton knew that he was the reason for the disconnect, so he was trying to be patient with Yogi. Whatever he had to do to get back in her good graces was what he would do. Especially since he was feeling guilty about the liking that she had taken to Caleb.

"The rep said someone will be here at eleven."

"Sounds good. What do you say we grab lunch after that? No Caleb, no Khristian, Imani, or King. Just me and my wife. What do you say?" Carlton actually sounded hopeful, but Yogi didn't care. She had no desire to have lunch with him, but she had to play the part until she found out what she needed to find out. Yogi didn't want to give Carlton a reason to suspect anything.

She finally put the mail down and looked at Carlton, which was a mistake. Yogi couldn't believe how she'd never seen it before. She never had a reason to think that Carlton had any connection to Caleb, but the resemblance was uncanny. The more she wanted to believe that she was just trippin', the tighter her chest began to feel. That woman's intuition had just kicked in, and Yogi wondered where in the hell it had been all along. She prided herself on being a smart woman, and while she knew who Carlton was, she really underestimated him and Imani. She took that girl in and treated her like family. The thought of Carlton in between the young woman's legs made Yogi want to throw up. Had she really been that blind and that stupid? Yogi counted to ten in her head to keep her temper at bay.

"Yes. We can go to lunch. That would be nice." She tried to put some emotion in her voice, but it was hard.

Carlton smiled and crossed the room. He grabbed Yogi's hand and looked lovingly into her eyes. "Let's put on some music and dance like we used to."

"I'm very tired, Carlton. Maybe another time." Yogi walked away, and Carlton stared after her, fuming.

This was the reason he cheated. Or at least that was the reason that he used to justify his cheating. Every time he tried to make love to his wife and be affectionate toward her lately, she rejected him. Carlton walked over to his minibar and grabbed a bottle of scotch. He sipped the strong, stiff drink with an attitude. He wanted to be climbing up in some pussy, but once again, he couldn't get any from the woman he was married to.

Carlton sat in the den drinking glass after glass of scotch, and soon, he was like a man with a vendetta. He stood up angrily and thought about going to the bedroom and demanding his wife give him some, but he didn't. Even in his drunken state, Carlton knew he could only take it so far with Yogi. She didn't play that bullshit, but he knew who he could try. Carlton snatched his keys up and left the house. If she wasn't going to sleep with him, Yogi wouldn't mind if he left back out of the house.

Carlton had paid the mortgage on his and Yogi's house until it was paid off. Now, he was paying rent at Imani's house. Carlton wasn't going to keep paying rent and going to bed with a dry dick. By the time he pulled up at Imani's apartment, he was damn near seeing double. But he saw what he needed to see. Imani was laughing and getting out of her car dressed in some short shorts and a white crop with some PINK slides on her feet. She had on a typical dick appointment outfit, and what made him even angrier was the fact that she didn't have Caleb with her. Carlton got out of his car and walked up to Imani, who gasped when she saw him.

"Carlton, what are you doing here?" she asked with one hand on her chest as if it would calm her racing heart.

"Where is my son?" Carlton's eyes were glassy, and she could smell the alcohol seeping through his pores.

"He's with a friend. What do you want?"

Carlton could tell that she was nervous, and to him that was an indication that she'd been up to no good. He didn't think about the fact that she had every reason to fear him after not one but two attempts on her life.

"What do I want?" Carlton's anger was evident, and Imani looked around, hoping and praying that someone was outside who could be a witness in case he tried anything. "Where have you been?"

Imani was still scared, but Carlton's nerve had her irritated as well. "Why does it matter? I've done everything that you asked me to do. I moved out of your house, I put Caleb on Red, and I haven't been bothering you."

"You haven't been bothering me? I pay your fucking rent. Every time I look up, you have Yogi babysitting your son like he's not her stepson. That shit is sick," he spat.

Imani shook her head. "Wow. Every time you look up, I have Yogi babysitting my son? He's your son too, or did you forget that? No, you didn't want me to have him, but my son was created out of love. During the time we messed around, you had sex with me more than you did Yogi. I wasn't just some lowly side chick you didn't have feelings for. You fucked me every chance you got. For the longest time not only did you have sex with me, but you sold me dreams."

"I sold you dreams?" Carlton spat. He was almost disgusted with himself for even getting caught up with the young woman. At the time, she stroked Carlton's ego and made him feel good, but she'd been more trouble than she was worth. He didn't even have the desire to have sex with her anymore. But he had just come up with an idea to kill two birds with one stone.

"How about I write you a check for two hundred and fifty thousand dollars if you do two things for me? First, help me handle something with Kareem, and afterward, take Caleb and leave town, and never come back."

Imani's eyes widened. This man was offering her $250,000 to help with some nigga and to leave town. The thought of that kind of money had her mouth watering. The Kareem thing was nothing, but where would she go? It would be hard to start over in a new city with a small child. The $250,000 would hold her over for a little while, but eventually she'd have to go back to work. Yogi's nonstop doting on Caleb and Khristian's frequent visits made Imani's life easy. Could she really leave town? What if she went to Atlanta or even Savannah, Georgia? Maybe she could go to Miami. Imani knew she had to think quickly on her feet.

"I want three hundred and fifty thousand. If I have to leave town and go to a place where I don't know anyone, that means I can't work right away because Caleb is still small, and I don't want him in day care. I'd have to stay home with him for at least two years, and I need money to live somewhere decent and take care of us. Now what is it you need my help on with Kareem?"

Carlton showcased an evil grin. "Nothing but what you are already doing. I just need you to keep it going, and when I call, you send him where I tell you to. Do that and you'll have your money in a week," he growled before walking off. He had to get his accountant to move some things around and make that large transaction look good in case Yogi started snooping.

Carlton headed toward his car without a clue in the world that he was being watched.

Yogi waited intently for Merrick to come pick her up. She had already gone out once without alerting him, and she knew that if King found out about it, he would be pissed, so today she was going to do what she was supposed to do. It had been about two hours since she and Carlton had their blood drawn, and Yogi was so anxious that she could barely think straight. It wasn't like her to be this out of whack, but she simply couldn't get it together. She was promised that the results would be rushed to her as soon as possible. Yogi was willing to pay whatever she needed to in order to have the results expedited. Per usual, Carlton left right after they had lunch. Yogi tried her best to act normal and not appear preoccupied, but she wasn't sure that she did a good job.

Carlton was used to it by now, and he was even starting to wonder if they should stay in their marriage. Even if he was the reason that Yogi was unhappy, why should they both be miserable? He was almost certain that he wanted out, and he knew she probably did too. She could keep the home, and he would continue to provide for her financially. It was on Carlton's mind heavy, but he didn't know how to bring it up to Yogi. Maybe he would be the one to let her bring it to him.

As soon as Merrick pulled up, Yogi grabbed her purse and walked out of the house. Merrick got out of the car and held the door open for Yogi. He could tell by her fast walk and the way she had her face twisted up that she was upset about something. "Good afternoon, Mrs. Yogi." He tipped his head at her.

"Hi," she stated with a frown still on her face.

Merrick wondered what was wrong, but he knew it wasn't really any of his business. He walked back around to his side and got in the vehicle. "Where to?" He looked over at her, and Yogi continued to stare straight ahead as she gave him an address downtown.

Merrick was resisting the urge to ask Yogi if she was okay. She was always nice to him no matter how much he remained emotionless and tried not to mix business and pleasure. Women liked for people to ask them how they were doing, but he just got the feeling that Yogi would suck him in deeper than he wanted to be sucked in. His last relationship had been many years ago, and his PTSD from the military and his many issues caused his relationship to end. Merrick spent many years drowning his sorrows in a bottle, and when he got tired of self-destructing, he went to therapy. Six months of therapy changed his life. Merrick got lonely sometimes, but he still wasn't sure he wanted to be in a relationship even though he was finally healed. Some days, he wanted someone to share his life with, and others, he felt that remaining alone would be best.

After ten minutes of being in the car, Merrick couldn't take the silence anymore. "You okay today, Mrs. Yogi? Seems like somebody pissed you off."

"I'm fine," she replied, still staring straight ahead. "Or at least I will be. Whatever I'm going through, I did it to myself. I knew who and what I was marrying when I did it. I messed up, and now I have to correct it."

Merrick raised his eyebrows as he drove, but he had no clue how to respond. Her words, however, let him know that he should have gone with his first mind to not get involved. He drove to the destination. Once they arrived, he got out and opened Yogi's door for her. It was customary for him to follow her inside, but something told him that she might want to do whatever she was about to do alone. King had paid him to do a job though, so he was going to go with her and keep his distance.

Merrick walked behind Yogi, admiring her red pantsuit and her black Louboutin heels. He followed her inside an office that belonged to a private investigator, and she checked in with the receptionist. The two sat in silence for ten minutes until Yogi was called to the back by a short dark-skinned man. Merrick figured she was safe with a private investigator in a place of business, so he remained in the waiting area.

Yogi walked to the back with her head held high. On the outside, she looked poised and confident, and on the inside, her mouth was dry, and she was nervous as hell. This wasn't even about Carlton anymore. If Caleb was his son, then that meant she had to cut ties with not only Imani but Caleb as well. Yogi would be cutting not one but three people from her life. Khristian would lose her friend. Life would be different for sure, and it would hurt. Yogi was a strong woman, but she was still human. As soon as she sat down, the private investigator spoke.

"At your request, I began my surveillance of your husband last night, and I was able to follow him to an apartment complex about nine miles from your home. That was the only place he went last night, and I have these pictures of the person he stood outside and talked to for a few moments."

He grabbed a manila folder, and Yogi held her breath while he pulled pictures out. He slid the photos across the desk, and Yogi didn't even have to pick them up. A rage so strong consumed her body, and she wanted to flip some shit over. He was at Imani's apartment. Something really was going on between them. "That sneaky little bitch." Tears filled Yogi's eyes. Carlton and Imani were as disrespectful as they came, and they were going to pay for that shit. Yogi looked through all three of the photos.

"They stood outside the entire time. He never went inside," the investigator stated as he saw the tears in Yogi's eyes.

"He may as well have." Yogi once again held her head high. "Thank you for getting on the job so quickly. You plan to watch him today, too?"

"I have eyes on him right now. The only reason I'm not doing it is because I'm meeting with you."

Yogi stood up. "Very well. Thank you so much for all of your help."

Her phone rang, and she pulled it from her bag. "Yes." It was the person who had drawn her and Carlton's blood, and Yogi wasn't even sure she was ready for the news, but it was now or never.

"Hi, Ms. Yogi. I just wanted to tell you that I ran three different tests, and they all just came back. Carlton is the father of the child whose mouth you swabbed."

Chapter Fifteen

King walked over to Kenny as he sat on a park bench. He really tried to let the shit that Sloan told him go, but he couldn't. King knew what had to be done when he had a nightmare about the shit. If he was having nightmares, he could only imagine what Sloan was going through. And now, Sloan had to relive the traumatic things that happened to her because these leeches wanted to pop up and beg. The sun was setting, and no one was around who King could see.

Kenny stood up when King approached. He was happier than a kid in a candy store. When King called him apologizing for Sloan's behavior at the party, Kenny breathed a sigh of relief. He had done his homework on King, too, and King had more money than Sloan. He didn't need that bitch if he could get on King's good side.

"What's going on, man?" King's skin felt like it was crawling when Kenny extended his hand, and he shook it. He had to play the part if only for a little while. "Again, I want to apologize for inviting you to the party. I didn't know Sloan was going to behave like that, but she's pregnant, and she's hormonal. She won't even talk to me about it, and I'm just assuming she's on that dramatic shit. What's the story with y'all?" King looked at the man inquisitively. He didn't need to hear Kenny's side of the story. He just needed to buy some time.

Kenny nervously scratched the back of his neck, and King knew a lie was about to fall off his lips. "Ah, man, we never really got along. She always felt like I was stealing her mother's attention from her. Once she got older and started going through puberty, she started wearing little shorts around me and whatnot. Trying her best to get the attention from me that she had lost. Her mom began to notice, and she got on Sloan about it. I guess Sloan was mad or embarrassed, and she started lying, saying that I was trying to sleep with her. She got mad when her mom didn't believe her, and she went as far as getting me locked up for the bogus shit. I forgive her though. She was a troubled, insecure kid."

King was so angry he was surprised that he wasn't foaming at the mouth. This nigga stood there and told a bald-faced lie with a straight face. King wanted to body Sloan's mother too, but Kenny would have to do. King gave a head nod, and Kenny thought that meant that King understood where he was coming from. He didn't know that was the signal that he was giving to Panama to come end his life. Kenny had just opened his mouth to tell another lie when a bullet to the head stopped his lies forever. Before his body could hit the ground, King had already turned and was walking away. This piece of shit would never be able to hurt Sloan again, and he couldn't wait to give her the news. Her mother was sure to be trying to up her scamming game now since her useless husband was dead, and King wouldn't hesitate to end her life either in an effort to protect Sloan's peace.

There wasn't anything he wouldn't do for her, and he needed her to know that. She had been quieter than usual since her party, and King knew that seeing her mother and stepfather made her feel some kind of way, and she was trying to hide it. King wanted her to know that she didn't have to front for him. Anything that was bothering her, he would do whatever was necessary to make it better for her. Inside the car, Panama spoke to King about the next order of business as if he hadn't just killed a man.

"We got the drop on two of Chin's little flunkies tonight. We're gonna hit them and take their product right before we take their lives," Panama assured him.

"Sounds like a plan to me."

The men went over specifics until Panama dropped King off at his car. King went to Sloan's house since she was only going to be in town for two more days before it was back out of town to work. Sloan's stomach was still flat, but her breasts were bigger, and her face was fuller. She looked amazing to King with the extra weight, but she was starting to freak out and feel insecure about her looks. No matter how many people assured her that she looked good, Sloan was always finding something to stress over, and she knew the pregnancy rumors would start soon. People had linked her to King and any other man they saw her near until her party. Once a few photos of her and King at the party got out, people pretty much knew that they were a couple. Sloan even drank sparkling apple cider at her party so people would think she was drinking champagne. If anyone saw her turning down alcohol, they'd really know that she was pregnant.

"Hey, baby," King said as Sloan opened the door. He pulled her into his arms and kissed her on the forehead. "That nigga is dead."

Sloan looked up at him with a confused look on her face. "Huh? Who is dead, King?"

"Your stepfather." He said it in a tone so cold that a shiver ran down Sloan's spine.

"How?" she asked, dumbfounded. She had an idea, but she didn't want to assume.

"I had Panama off that nigga. I had a nightmare about what that sick bastard did to you. And truthfully, the way he and your mom were acting, there's no doubt in my mind they were going to be coming with more bullshit as you get more successful. I'm not letting you walk around worried about when or where that sick muhfucka might come at you wrong. He had to go, and I don't regret that shit."

Sloan never thought she'd ever take a life, but she did in order to protect herself and her man. After she killed her ex, she only felt a small sense of relief, and she honestly hoped that she'd never have to kill again, but Sloan wasn't that same scared child. She would have killed Kenny before she ever let him touch her again, but she was in a small way glad that King had handled it for her. Sloan absolutely hated Kenny's guts. She almost felt ashamed when the news made her melt in King's arms. Sloan's body relaxed, and she knew she was safe with him. They shared a silent moment for what felt like the longest time. Sloan didn't even know what to say, but she felt good in King's arms.

He was the one to break the silence. "Are you feeling okay?" he pulled back and looked at her.

"I feel fine, and I feel even better when you're here." Sloan gazed into King's eyes, and she silently prayed that he understood what she meant. And he did.

"Baby, I'm gon' be here always. I have my people wrapping up any problems that we have now, and after that, I'm done. I'm out of the game, and I'm just focusing on you, our baby, and the label. I'm walking away from all this shit."

Sloan was relieved, but she was too afraid to get prematurely happy. She knew that anything could happen, but all she could do was hope and pray that King would make it out of the game unscathed. "Promise?"

"I promise, baby." King's deep voice and his strong arms wrapped around her made Sloan feel all the comfort in the world. She chose to believe that things would work out the way that she wanted them to.

"I love you."

"I love you too," King admitted. He had never spoken those words with so much emotion to a woman who wasn't family, but he meant it with Sloan. He grabbed her hand and walked her over to the couch. He was waiting to get word from Panama that the hit on Chin's men had been successful. Once that was done, he'd be another step closer to ending his run in the game.

King headed into the restaurant at his mother's request. When he arrived, he peeped Merrick parked in the cut, and he was glad that Yogi wasn't fighting him about having security. Upon entering the restaurant, he saw his mother sitting near the back with a tight-lipped expression on her face. He could tell right away that she was upset, and he wondered what was wrong. When the hostess offered to seat him, he made her aware that he was there for Yogi. She led him toward the table. King and Yogi locked eyes, and he saw that something was terribly wrong with his mother, and that made him anxious. King would move heaven and earth for his mother. Whoever it was who had pissed Yogi off had better be hiding. King kissed his mother on the cheek and sat down across from her.

"What's going on?" He wanted to get right down to business.

"Carlton. He's Caleb's father." Yogi wasn't being the strong, confident woman King knew. She looked fragile and vulnerable, and King didn't like that shit. Aside from not liking to see his mother upset, King was perturbed at the news that he'd just heard.

"What?"

"The day you came to the house and joked about Caleb looking like Carlton was a red flag for me. It's like I was seeing him for the first time, and all of a sudden, all I saw when I looked at him was my husband. I went and bought an at-home DNA test, and I swabbed his mouth. I then tricked Carlton into giving a blood sample. I also had a private investigator following him, and he went to Imani's apartment. This entire fucking time that whore was fucking my husband. After I invited her into my home. After I treated that child like my own. She and Carlton played in my motherfucking face. Do you know how hard it was not to tear that fucking house up?" Yogi was furious, and King was amazed that she had held her composure for that long. He himself was stunned at the news.

King knew that Caleb resembled Carlton, but he really said the shit as a joke, and he was confused. "So, the entire time we've been looking for Imani's baby daddy, it was Carlton?" King was dumbfounded. "I knew her pinning that shit on Red sounded iffy as fuck."

"That also explains why her story all of a sudden switched up. She didn't lie when she said he was older and married. King, that little bitch stood in my house and played in my fucking face. I'm beating her ass for this one, and no one can talk me out of it. I mean that shit."

King wouldn't dare try to talk his mother out of beating Imani's ass. Anyone that bold would have to deal with whatever came their way.

"So, Carlton was the one who possibly killed Tiana?" King didn't want to believe it. Him being Caleb's father was messed up, but if he was really responsible for Tiana's death, whether he meant to do it or not, Kareem would feel he had to go. And that was unfortunate because Carlton had been in King's life for so long.

"It makes sense." Yogi leaned forward. "Carlton might have the audacity to step out on me and stick his dick in random places, but do you think he wanted her to have that baby? Her ass got pushed down the stairs while pregnant, and a bomb was planted underneath her car. That seems like a person going through drastic measures to me."

"Wow." King had seen a lot of shit in his day, and still, he was stunned. "You know if I tell Kareem this shit, it's a wrap."

"Honestly, between me and Kareem, I'm not sure which one of us will end Carlton's life first," Yogi replied coldly.

King didn't want to feel soft, but all the bodies were finally starting to take a toll on him. Plus, no matter what, Carlton was like his father. True, the Caleb situation was fucked up, but it was not justification for ending his life. Now the Tiana deal was something different, and if King was going to get behind Kareem on that, he needed 100 percent proof that it was Carlton.

"I don't give a fuck. When that motherfucker is dead, I'll be even richer than I am now. I say good fucking riddance and do it fast. It's so hard living in the same house with that man and having to act like everything is okay. I just ask one thing. I want to be there. I want to look him in the face and see how he reacts when he knows that I know."

King nodded. "Okay, Mom, just promise me before you do or say anything, let me get all my ducks in a row. Let's not forget that he's Khristian's father and your husband."

Yogi drew back. "Carlton is already dead to me. Fuck that disrespectful-ass nigga, but on my baby love for him, I'll hold my peace until it's time. But as for that li'l bitch, Imani has to see me. There's no way on earth I'm letting that shit slide."

King nodded. Yogi looked certain about what she wanted to do to that young girl, and King wasn't really surprised. Imani had done the unthinkable, and the shit was right up under their noses. This entire time they'd been comingling with the enemy and didn't even know it.

He had invited Imani to all family meetings and offered her protection along with his mother and sister, and the whole time she was a scandalous-ass bird. She didn't even flinch when it came to putting her son on a dead man. King didn't give a fuck about Red, but her actions showed him just how callous Imani was. She knew who was out to get her and who was responsible for Tiana's death, but to put Carlton on blast would be to tell on herself. King was disgusted. This was some sick shit, and he couldn't respect it.

He really didn't even have an appetite, and neither did Yogi, so they ordered some drinks, and King paid the tab and left a tip. As he walked his mother to her car, all he could do was shake his head. It seemed as if the killing wouldn't be slowing up anytime soon.

Chapter Sixteen

"I'm really sorry about what happened last time. You have really been here for us."

Imani looked up at Kareem, and he seemed truly sorry. She had come over again to sit with the kids while Kareem had to run out.

"Like I told you, Reem, I will always be here for you and the kids as long as I'm able."

Kareem nodded. "I appreciate that, and I promise I'm going to make it all up to you when this is all over."

Imani and Kareem stared at each other, and no words were spoken for a brief moment. There was definitely a chemistry starting to form. But Imani knew that it was too late. She had already agreed to help Carlton, and it looked like getting rid of Kareem was on his mind. She wasn't positively sure what he had planned, but he was paying and working hard to know Kareem's whereabouts.

The sound of him clearing his throat broke the silence. "I'll be back in like an hour and a half."

"Okay. I'll just sit here and catch up on some reading."

As soon as Kareem was out the door, Imani jumped on the phone and let Carlton know that he was leaving the house. Carlton had already set up a face-to-face with Kareem, telling him he had some new information on Texas's and Chin's locations and they needed to move on it immediately. The truth of the matter was that Carlton had spoken with them and let them know that if Kareem was dealt with, the war could be over and they all could get back to business. With King getting out of the game, Carlton would be running things, and he had agreed to split corners and trap houses with them.

Kareem tore himself away from staring at Imani, and he left the house. King had been talking a lot about leaving the game, and Kareem was going to be right there with his ass. Working for the record label would be stressful at times also, but it would be nothing like the dope game with unpredictable hours and unforeseen dangers.

"Damn, baby," Kareem mumbled as he drove down the street. "You supposed to be here with me. We supposed to be raising these kids together and having nasty-ass sex every night." Many days, Kareem started to do what Tiana's mother asked and let the kids come live with her, but he felt that would be taking the easy way out. He wanted to get that single father thing down pat and show his kids that he'd never give up on them. More than ever, he had to salute Tiana for always holding shit down whether he was around or not. She made motherhood look easy, but he felt like he was drowning. He missed her so fucking bad that it hurt.

Kareem pulled a blunt from his ashtray and lit it when he came to a stop at a red light. After taking a deep pull and going through the green light, he heard loud popping sounds. It took him a brief moment to register what was happening, and by that time, he heard glass shattering and felt a hot bullet penetrating his arm, then his chest, then his shoulder. Kareem mashed the gas and took off as the various bullets caused him great pain. He got caught slipping and was now trying to drive away from the bullets with multiple injuries. Blood soaked his shirt as he sped down the road. Kareem was fifteen minutes away from the nearest hospital, and he knew he'd surely bleed out before he arrived.

Kareem gritted his teeth and gripped the steering wheel as the pain intensified, and he began to feel light-headed. His foot involuntarily relaxed, and he ran up on a curb and hit a light pole. Kareem's head rested on the seat as he stared at the sky through the windshield. His arm was numb, and he no longer felt any pain. He was just cold. So cold that he was shivering. He almost smiled at the thought of Tiana. If he was about to die, then just maybe he might see her again, even though he was a hell-bound type of nigga and he figured Tiana would be in heaven for sure. He still clung to the hope that maybe they could be together in the afterlife, but as his eyes began to feel heavy and his lids closed, Kareem thought about his three kids.

His shorties would be fucked up for sure if they lost both him and Tiana. All he could do was hope that Tiana's mother would raise his kids and treat them well. He knew they'd be good financially as long as there was breath in King's body. Kareem began to drift off into darkness.

Chapter Seventeen

King watched Sloan from backstage with admiration. Despite having thrown up two hours before her show, she had been on stage for the past thirty minutes killing it, and she had his undivided attention. King was not only happy that his business investment was a success, but he was happy that this was the woman he was deciding to live life with. King had been so focused and busy that he didn't have time to entertain random women, and it was then that he realized he didn't want to. King no longer wanted to get head or have sex with every cute female with a fat ass. Life had become so much bigger than that. Sloan was having his child, and he wanted to do right by her.

Once she finished the set, she walked off stage with a smile on her face, and King picked her up and twirled her around. He no longer cared about keeping their relationship a secret. She would only be able to hide her pregnancy for another few months, and that was only if no one behind the scenes ran their mouth. Photographers, makeup artists, stylists, studio engineers, et cetera had all seen Sloan throw up or not feel good. There was some minor weight gain, and she always turned down alcohol. There was a chance that someone would want to be the first one to spill the tea and sell the information to a gossip blog, but so far no one had said anything. At least King didn't think so.

"King, you're going to make me throw up," Sloan giggled, and King placed her on her feet.

"You did an amazing job tonight, babe. I am so proud of you." The sincerity in King's eyes and the way he was gazing at her made Sloan blush. Everything about King made her feel like a schoolgirl inside, a giddy schoolgirl crushing on the most popular nigga at the school. But King was a grown-ass man, and he definitely made her feel like a grown-ass woman.

"Thank you, but I am so exhausted. I just want to get home and get in the bed."

"Let's go then." King grabbed Sloan's hand and led her through the small crowd back to her dressing room. The show she did was forty-five minutes away from home, and he knew she'd probably be asleep as soon as she got in the car.

Inside the dressing room, King watched Sloan change her clothes and wash the makeup off her face. He made sure that her room had been set up with everything she needed to be comfortable. There were mad bottles of water out along with sour candy. Sloan had learned that sucking on sour candy sometimes helped her nausea, and since then, King made sure to always have some on deck for her no matter where they were. With the loud music gone and him not being preoccupied, King realized that his phone was vibrating in his pocket. He hadn't looked at his phone in hours, and when he finally did, he saw that he had seventeen missed calls. He immediately began to worry. He had missed calls from Tiana's mother, Yogi, Panama, and Khristian. After some quick evaluating, he saw that he had no missed calls from Kareem, so it was either an immediate family issue that maybe Kareem didn't know about, or it was concerning Kareem.

"What's up?" he answered his mother's fifth call of the night.

"King, I know you're at the show with Sloan, but, baby, Kareem is dead." Yogi's voice was filled with pain, and King knew that this was something that she knew for sure and not just a rumor. He still had to try his hand, however.

"Yeah, right. What are you talking about, Ma? Who told you this? I'm about to call and get this straightened out."

Hearing him so adamant and confident that it was bullshit further broke Yogi's heart. His denial was something that she didn't want to have to prove to him was wrong. Yogi wished she were wrong, but she wasn't.

"King, baby, I know for sure. The police called his mother. His identification was in the car. They know it was him. He was shot. There were more than ten shell casings in the street, he was hit three times, and his car hit a pole. Kareem is gone, King. I'm so sorry."

King's breathing was restricted. Sloan was all done and ready to go, but as soon as she turned and looked at King, she knew something was wrong. He looked as if he'd seen a ghost. The way he clutched his phone in his hand and held it up to his ear while he had a vacant look in his eyes made her aware that someone had called him with bad news, and her heart sank. What in the world was wrong now? Foolishly, Sloan had gotten comfortable with not hearing any bad news for the past few days, and she hoped all of the drama was dying down.

"Ma, I gotta go. I'll hit you back." King barely recognized his own voice, so he cleared his throat as if that would help. He ended the call and looked at Sloan. "You ready?"

King had already seen one of his friends die. He literally held him while he took his last fuckin' breath. Now the same fucked-up game had claimed the life of Kareem. There were three children who had lost both of their parents weeks apart, and that shit wasn't fair.

Sloan placed her palm against his chest. "King, what's wrong? Tell me."

He didn't want to repeat the words. That would make it too real. King felt like he was floating through a fog. Everything around him was just noise. He couldn't focus on anything. It felt as if the air were leaving his lungs. Death was inevitable in the streets, but not Kareem. They had beaten the odds too many times. They had come out on top so many times that King expected it this time as well. They lost Tiana, but that was it. That was as bad as it was going to get. Or so he thought.

When King wouldn't speak, Sloan became very concerned. "Baby, please."

"Kareem is dead. Sloan, we gotta go." King turned to leave. He couldn't talk about it.

Sloan's mouth fell open as she watched him walk away. She wanted to go after him, but her legs wouldn't move. It was as if she forgot how to walk. This was hitting too close to home. First Tiana and now Kareem. King would normally never forget to grab her hand and guide her safely through a room of people. That was when Sloan knew he was out of it, and she didn't hold it against him. He already disappeared, and she knew that both of them couldn't be stuck. Sloan remembered how to use her legs and hurried out of the room after him.

King ignored every person calling out to him, trying to talk to him, and taking pictures. He had tunnel vision toward the exit. It wasn't until he spotted security standing by the door ready to escort him out that he turned back to look for Sloan. He didn't see her at first, and he cursed under his breath. "Fuck." He assumed she was behind him, and he just left her. He was about to go back when he spotted her coming toward him. As soon as she was within earshot, he began to apologize.

"I'm sorry, Sloan. I thought you were behind me."

"You don't have to apologize to me. I'm sorry for walking so slow. Come on, let's get you to your family."

King grabbed her hand, and he appreciated how she was taking charge and being supportive because he needed it. She kept her grip on his hand well after they got in the car and were on their way. King stared out of the window, and all of the memories that he had of him and Kareem played in his mind like a movie. King had taken so many losses that it was on the verge of driving him insane. This shit had to stop. He couldn't consult Carlton, he couldn't go to Kareem, but he was going to the members of his team who were left. King wouldn't sleep until this shit was rectified. He was going to get Sloan somewhere safe and out of sight. He was canceling any interviews or work that she had until this shit with Chin was done.

When he turned to her and explained that, to his surprise, she didn't object. Sloan was nervous her damn self, and she wouldn't argue with being out of harm's way. Her single was doing awesome, her fan base was growing daily, she was even on the Billboard Hot 100 singles chart. Sloan's career had already surpassed what she had ever dreamed of. She now knew that she could be a successful singer, and even though she had so much more to accomplish, she was no longer afraid or skeptical. She crossed so many goals off her list. There was nothing wrong with her slowing down for a bit and letting King handle his business.

"Okay, babe. Whatever you want. I'm fine with that."

King's world had been turned upside down, and he was so glad that Sloan was making this as easy as possible for him and not fighting him on anything. He began to send out text messages and emails clearing her schedule and getting her a penthouse suite set up in one of the city's best hotels. King gave Sloan her hotel accommodations.

"I'll have a shopper go to pick up everything that you'll need. The hotel will have bathrobes, slippers, and things like that, but I'll have a week's worth of clothes delivered to you. Don't open your door for anyone except hotel staff, Mona, Merrick, or Panama."

Sloan nodded. Shit was getting real, but they couldn't just wait and be sitting ducks. King was taking action, and she was going to pray harder than she ever had before that King would make it out of this alive. At the hotel, King and security walked Sloan up to her room, and he kissed her goodbye. Before he could turn to leave, Sloan grabbed his hand. It wasn't the time to show fear or be weak.

"You will go handle your business and make it back to me and our baby." Her heart was beating fast in her chest, and that let her know how afraid she was, but Sloan appeared as confident as possible for her man.

"I'm definitely coming back to you," he promised and kissed her with enough passion to make her vagina throb for him. Sloan wanted to go in the room and make love to him in case that ended up being the last time, but there was no time for that. King had business to handle.

Chapter Eighteen

Ron and Texas stood outside of Donna's house, talking. A few of Chin's trap houses had been hit days before, and he was livid and ordering them to get rid of King once and for all. Carlton's promise that with Kareem gone everything would cease was not happening. It looked like it had actually only made things worse. King was now looking for blood only.

"We need to get at this King nigga. Kareem is dead now, so it shouldn't be too hard to hit that nigga."

"Yeah, I been trying to get his stepfather to give him up, but he not with it," Ron said before he smirked.

Texas grinned. "Maybe we can get the bitch Imani to help us. She knows the sister, and if we can kidnap her, you know the nigga going to put on his cape and try to come save her. Once we off that nigga and get him out of the picture, we can take out Carlton ass, too, and get all the money. Call her and let her know what's up." Texas was ready to wrap their meeting up and get back in the crib to slide up in some of Donna's tight-ass pussy. The two had been fucking like rabbits lately. She was definitely worth every dime that Texas had spent on her.

Ron pulled his phone from his pocket to call Imani, but he never got to dial the number. The men heard tires screeching, and they looked up at the same time. They didn't even have time to pull their guns out as bullets started flying. A black car was speeding down the street, and the passenger side windows were down in the front and the back. Two men hung from the car window spraying semiautomatic weapons, and Texas and Ron were both shot before they even knew what hit them. Ron was hit so many times that by the time his body hit the ground he resembled Swiss cheese. King had his men go out with a vengeance, and everybody affiliated with the opposing side was being dealt with.

Inside the house, Donna heard the succession of bullets, and she hit the floor. She flinched as glass from her windows rained down on the carpet and bullets hit the side of her house. It sounded like cannons were being let loose. She knew that Texas was out in the yard talking to Ron, and unless he hit the ground fast as fuck, she was afraid that he wouldn't make it out of the line of fire. It felt like she was on the floor forever, but it was really less than a minute. Even after the shooting stopped, Donna lay on the floor for a bit, trying to get herself together. Thank God she wasn't hit, but her joy was short-lived. She remembered that Texas was outside, and she hopped up off the floor. She yanked the front door open and ran out onto the porch. Her eyes fell on Texas and Ron laid out in her front yard bleeding profusely, and she screamed. Neither of them was moving, and their eyes were closed. Seeing all the blood and all the bullet holes, she knew there was no way they were alive. People ran out of their homes to see what was going on, and all Donna could do was stand there and scream. The murder and mayhem in the streets of Charlotte continued.

Chin could barely see. His eyes were almost swollen shut. His breathing was shallow, and he was on the verge of passing out from the pain. His ribs had to be broken because every time he inhaled a breath it felt like he was dying. He damn near wished he could stop breathing.

That was how bad it was. He put up a good fight when niggas killed two of his henchmen and ran up on him trying to grab him. Because Chin put up such a good fight, Panama and Merrick beat the brakes off his ass, damn near killing him. But they couldn't kill him just yet. They were going to leave that task for King.

Even though his vision was far from good with the state that his eyes were in, Chin could see King enter the room clear enough. King had seen better days himself. It had been two days since Kareem was killed, and King's beard was already looking like that of an unkempt man. It needed to be shaped up, his eyes were bloodshot red, and he had bags underneath them. Kareem's death had fucked him up, and seeing Chin take his last breath was the only thing that would bring him the smallest amount of pleasure.

"Bitch-ass nigga," King sneered as he walked up on a barely breathing Chin. "You had your men to kill my nigga, and for that shit, I was gon' let my niggas carve you up like a turkey, but I don't have the time for all of that. I'm just going to put a bullet in between your eyes and get this shit over with."

Like King, Chin was no stranger to death. The game was full of it. He knew there was no way in hell that they were going to let him go, so he smiled, showcasing his blood-tinged teeth.

"That wasn't just on me. You can add your step-pops and his little girlfriend. Couldn't have done it without them." Chin knew exactly what he was doing. He knew it was no way he was making it out alive, but being help to divide King's family brought him his last bit of joy.

King couldn't believe what he was hearing, but the last few days had proven that anything was possible. Turning his attention back to Chin, King aimed the gun at his head. "Any last words?"

Chin smiled and spoke, "Fuck you!" He used the last bit of his energy to utter those words to King, and they would be his last.

King blacked out and pumped bullet after bullet into Chin until his clip was empty. King was exhausted, so he didn't even have to tell Panama and Merrick what to do. They already knew. He was damn near seeing double when he got in the back seat of the Tahoe he was in.

"Where to, boss?" the driver asked.

"Take me home," King stated in a gruff voice.

Imani got Caleb out of the car, and they headed up Yogi's driveway. She had been going crazy all last night. She hadn't heard from Carlton since she had let him know when Kareem was leaving. The shooting had been all over the news and social media. Sitting there watching the photos of Kareem's car full of bullet holes had her feeling kind of guilty. She didn't exactly know Carlton had plans on killing Kareem, and had she, a part of her felt like she wouldn't have helped him. But on the other hand, she had more than given Kareem the opportunity to wife her up, but his ass was taking too long and still mourning Tiana's death. So Imani felt like she had to do what was best for her and Caleb.

Now her biggest problem was Carlton. She had no way of being sure if he was really going to give her the money that he promised. She was well familiar with how he was after getting what he wanted. Imani was anxious, and her nerves were getting the best of her. Yogi had called and asked her over, saying she missed Caleb and that, in this time of grief, family needed to be together. That made Imani breathe a sigh of relief, that she was still considered family. She didn't hesitate to take Caleb by to visit Yogi, because then she might be able to get the tea on what was up with Carlton. Imani wanted her money, and his ass better not try to back out.

Yogi answered the door with a smile on her face and immediately took the baby from Imani's arms. Yogi played with Caleb for a few minutes while Imani made herself comfortable on the couch. Yogi walked over to Caleb's swing and placed him in it. She then walked over to where Imani was and started beating her ass. She definitely knew something, there was no doubt in Imani's mind. Yogi had a mean grip on her hair with one hand and was beating her face in with the other. Imani was so caught off guard and the blows were coming so fast that she really couldn't fight back. She attempted to swing up, but she wasn't connecting. She was sitting down, and Yogi was standing, whooping her ass. She hit Imani over and over again until all she could see were spots dancing before her eyes. Yogi even took it back to the old school and talked to Imani while she was beating her.

"You disrespectful-ass slut bucket. You deserve a bullet to the head instead of an ass whooping, you trifling-ass whore." Yogi dragged Imani off the couch, and her butt hit the floor with a hard thud, but that pain was nothing compared to the closed-fist blows she was receiving.

She then dragged the woman through the living room and into the kitchen. Imani kicked and cried as Yogi beat her like she'd never been beaten in her life. After another two minutes, Yogi's fist was throbbing, and she was out of breath. She finally stopped hitting Imani, and she let her hair go, but she kicked the woman in the side. Imani's head was pounding, her nose was bleeding, she could taste blood in her mouth, and her side felt like it had been stomped in. Imani wanted to get up off the floor so badly, but she couldn't. Her ass was hurt and embarrassed. Ass whooping was an understatement for the brutal attack that had just happened to her.

"I was going to kill you," Yogi made her aware. "But your son saved your life. After looking into Caleb's eyes, I couldn't kill you."

"Mrs. Yogi, I'm so sorry. I was stupid, and I know that now, but I had no idea that he was going to kill Kareem. Really I didn't." Imani gasped as pain radiated through her chest.

Yogi's breathing almost stopped. "What the fuck are you talking about? What did he have to do with what happened to Kareem?"

Imani, now realizing that Yogi didn't know everything, knew she had fucked up again, but after that ass whooping she wasn't about to cover again for Carlton's ass. She told Yogi everything.

Afterward, Imani sat on the floor and cried until Yogi snapped at her.

"You being honest now is the only thing that will stop me from letting King kill you. Now get your stupid, pathetic ass up off my floor. Get that bastard-ass baby and get the fuck out my house. Every time I see you, ho, I'm beating your ass. I don't care if I see you in church," Yogi promised, and she was dead serious.

Even with the shame and the pain that came with Yogi assaulting her, Imani was still grateful to be alive. She had spent enough time with the family to know some of their most intimate secrets, and there was no mystery about how they got down. They could be ruthless as fuck and very violent. The fact that Yogi let her live said a lot, and Imani wanted to get out of there before the woman changed her mind. With a great deal of shame making her sore body burn, Imani sniffled as she walked over to Caleb and got him out of his swing.

Carlton sat at his desk with his hands clasped together as if he were praying. He wasn't talking to God, however.

He was just staring off into space. His mind was wandering between the money he was going to be making with Chin and the renewed love he was planning to form with Yogi. Carlton only had one problem: Imani. He just wanted her to go far away, and a part of him doubted that she would do just that. Something was telling him that Imani would leave for a little bit to appease him, but then she'd be back in his damn hair, getting on his nerves and threatening his new life. With what he was planning with Yogi, he didn't need Imani coming along and messing it up.

Carlton was still in deep thought when his phone rang. He saw that it was King calling him, and he didn't hesitate to answer. "What's going on, son?"

"I need to see you ASAP. It's an emergency. I need you to come to the spot."

Carlton knew all too well where the spot was, and he knew, where serious matters were concerned, King couldn't and wouldn't talk over the phone. It was late, but he wouldn't hesitate to go. He figured this would be the meetup about taking revenge for Kareem's death. Carlton already had his speech planned out. He was going to try to talk King down on ramping up this already bloody street war with Chin. Too many bodies had already dropped, and dropping more was going to bring too much unwanted attention to the drug game, attention that none of them needed, especially King, since he was trying to exit the game into the music industry. With Kareem gone, it was time to end it. He was really the one keeping it going in the first place. Carlton was going to suggest a sit-down and new terms. Terms that he had already made with Chin, in truth. King would have to see that this beef was a broke man's sport, slowing him from the new life he had waiting.

"I'll be there in twenty minutes."

"I appreciate you."

Carlton got up and left to go see what it was that King needed. He would worry about Imani at a later time.

When Carlton arrived at the designated meeting spot, he walked inside and was very surprised to see Yogi there. Panama sat at King's side, and all eyes were on Carlton. "What's going on?" he asked, looking from King to Panama and then Yogi. Yogi being there was what stood out to him the most.

There was silence for a brief moment, and then Yogi spoke. "You're a lowlife piece of shit, that's what's going on. Out of all the underhanded bullshit that you have ever done, this is the worst." Yogi's eyes were glossed over with rage, and Carlton knew this shit was serious.

Imani had to have opened her big-ass mouth. He hadn't done anything else for Yogi to be this upset over, he thought. Carlton was a strong alpha male, but the way that King and Panama were glaring at him almost made him nervous. He didn't break character though. He simply looked at Yogi with a face full of confusion. "What are you talking about?"

She walked over to Carlton and slapped him in the face so hard that her hand stung. Carlton was caught off guard and damn near ready to slap her back, but he remembered where he was. King and Panama were looking like they were ready to pounce if he made one wrong move, and that let Carlton know that shit was serious. No matter what problems he and Yogi had in the past, she had never involved King in their shit. Their problems stayed in the house behind closed doors.

"You had me babysitting your bastard-ass child!" Yogi was so mad that she was shaking, and Carlton knew that she truly knew. She was too pissed to be speculating. She knew some shit for sure, and he'd never be able to make her feel like she wasn't accurate. "You had me taking care of that child. You and Imani crossed a line, and you can't ever come back from it. You did me dirtier than anyone has ever done me in my fucking life." Yogi's voice cracked, but she didn't cry. "You are a fucking piece of shit, and Imani is a fucking whore. The both of you stood in my house and played me for a fucking fool."

Carlton's heart started racing, and he knew Yogi wasn't a fool, but he had to try something. "It's not what you think. I admit I fucked up once. I was drunk, and she seduced me. I didn't know that was my child. She moved into our house to be vindictive. She told me that was Red's baby, but she gave you all this bullshit about the father being older and married. I asked her what kind of games she was playing. You have to believe me, Yogi." Carlton was pleading.

"You are the reason that Tiana is dead, and you went to the funeral. You sat up like family, and the entire time you knew you were the reason behind that shit. But really I could have forgiven you for all that, but Kareem? That man took a charge to get locked up with me. His loyalty to me and mine has been unmatched over the years, and you set him up?" King growled with tears in his eyes. "You got to die, nigga!"

"That wasn't me." Carlton's voice wasn't confident at all, and that was a first for him.

The men had never seen him unsure or anxious about anything. His fear was a dead giveaway that he was in fact the one responsible for Tiana's and Kareem's deaths, and King wanted blood. Stepfather or not, he had to die.

King pulled his pistol and cocked it. He was seething.

Carlton saw the gun and panicked. A thin layer of sweat covered his forehead, and his eyes darted between King and Yogi.

"Please don't do this. We're family. Son, please."

King frowned up his face. "Nah, I'm not your son. But you are my sister's father, and I couldn't look her in the face if I killed your sorry ass. Panama, put this mutherfucker out of his misery," King spoke.

Carlton looked back at Panama, and as soon as their eyes locked, Panama pulled the trigger back-to-back and sent multiple bullets into Carlton's body. Carlton's body hit the floor, and King walked over and stood over him. As Carlton gargled blood and looked up at King with scared eyes, King sent another bullet through Carlton's head and put him out of his misery. Carlton was dead, and King, Yogi, and Panama looked on without feeling any sympathy. They all at one time had love for the man, but no more.

Merrick entered the room so quietly that Yogi didn't even hear him. He didn't want to speak and startle her, so he just admired her for a moment. He cleared his throat to announce his presence, and Yogi turned slowly to face him. She was still in shock about what Carlton and Imani had done, and most days, she would spend what felt like hours just staring off into space. She was hurt and betrayed, and losing Kareem was an additional knife in her heart. "Hi. I didn't hear you come in."

"I've mastered the art of being able to enter a room without being heard. It comes in handy in my line of work. Are you good?" Merrick was tired and ready to get home, but he had to check on Yogi first.

Yogi let out a deep sigh, and he could tell that she was troubled. "I will be fine. If there's one thing I've learned in my life, it's that there isn't anything I can't bounce back from."

"You got that right. You are a very strong woman, and I know you can overcome anything. This whole thing with King is being wrapped up."

"I hope so. My son has been talking about leaving the game, and I want that for him more than anything. He's about to have a child of his own, and after everything I've been through, getting that call that something happened to him would literally kill me."

Merrick could see the pain and the fear in Yogi's eyes.

"Kareem was like a son to me, and this situation has devastated me."

"That case will be cold soon enough. I'm sure of that."

Yogi nodded. She was just ready for all of this to be over, for her heart to heal, and to move on with her life.

She even missed Caleb, and that hurt, too. Carlton let her get attached to that child knowing who he was. It wasn't Caleb's fault, but Yogi would never do Imani's ho ass any favors by doing anything else for that baby. She would never babysit him again while Imani went and popped her pussy to the highest bidder. Khristian said that she heard Imani had started stripping, and Yogi almost regretted not killing her, but fuck her. Imani was dead to her, and even though it hurt, so was Caleb.

"Thank you for all that you've done for this family." Yogi nodded her head at Merrick. "You are appreciated."

Carlton had barely been dead for three days, but Merrick didn't care. Yogi wasn't sad about that man's death, and soon, he hoped that his business with King would be done. Once that was the case, he no longer had to worry about blurring the lines between personal and business. "Maybe I'll see you next time you have Sunday dinner."

Yogi was sharp enough to catch the subtle flirting. She wasn't the type who needed a man. After being married to Carlton for so long, she was almost looking forward to being single, and she would never marry again. Yogi would never again let a nigga play her for the fool, and she meant that, but she wasn't dead. There was nothing wrong with having a little fun, so after licking her lips, she smiled at Merrick.

"I'm going to hold you to that."

Chapter Nineteen

King opened his eyes and looked up at the ceiling. After the long week he had, he went home, showered, and entered the deepest sleep of his life. He wasn't aware of how long he'd been asleep, but he finally felt rested. His heart was still heavy, and that wouldn't go away for a long time, but he never had to worry about his family's safety ever again. King was officially done with the streets. He was no longer a drug dealer. He wanted no part of the game or the shit that came with it.

He got out of bed, showered, and went downstairs to make some breakfast. After he ate, King hit the barbershop to get a haircut and his beard trimmed and lined up, and the next stop was his favorite jeweler. King was finally on his way to the hotel that Sloan had been staying at. He hadn't had a lot of communication with her since he left her there, and he was sorry for that.

King got on the elevator and headed up to the top floor. He knocked on the door and waited for Sloan to answer. When she did, his heart swelled with pride. She had on a sweatsuit. There was no makeup on her face, and her hair was pulled up in a messy bun, but she looked beautiful, and most importantly, she looked refreshed.

When she saw King looking good and refreshed, she smiled and ran into his arms for a hug. She was so happy and relieved that he did in fact make it back to her. She wanted to cry, but she held it together. The relief that she felt was so intense. He kissed her lips repeatedly, and then Sloan got the shock of her life when he got down on one knee. Sloan gasped when King opened the blue ring box he pulled from his pocket and flipped the lid up. Inside was the biggest, clearest diamond that she had ever seen in her life. The rock was so big that her knees buckled.

"I am officially out of the game. I have plenty of staff to run the label for me. I want to take a year-long vacation and just watch you do your thing while I become a father and a husband. I love you so much. Will you marry me?"

Sloan nodded her head up and down profusely. She couldn't even give him a verbal yes because she was crying so hard. All of her dreams had come true. Her career was taking off. She was actually pretty famous. Sloan had even started therapy so the events of her childhood would no longer haunt her. She wanted to be healed by the time she had a child of her own so she would be the best mother that she could be. Now, she was going to be someone's wife, and that someone was rich, powerful, and no longer in the game. There was nothing more that she could ask for.

King slid the ring on her finger, stood up, and kissed her on the lips. "I can't wait to get you home and slide up in that, but first, there is something that I have to do. Grab your things."

Sloan didn't ask any questions. She just obliged her man. She got her belongings, then followed him out to the waiting car. Sloan laid her head on King's shoulder and enjoyed the moment. The sounds of H.E.R. played on the radio, and in her head, she was already planning the wedding. Sloan was surprised when they ended up in a cemetery of all places, but she didn't ask any questions. Once they were out of the car, King grabbed her hand and led her to a grave. As soon as she read the headstone, she knew it was his biological father's grave.

"Pops, I made it. I made it out. I escaped prison, and I escaped death. Your son did it. I've taken too many losses, and none of them were worth it. I'll never get over losing you, and I don't want to do that to my child. This is Sloan. The love of my life, the mother of my child, and my future wife. I did good, Pop, and I'm looking after, too."

Sloan squeezed his hand, and they stood in silence. The King of the South was no more.

Also Available

The Cartel:

20 Year Anniversary Edition

Prologue

"Diamonds are forever." —Carter Diamond

The packed courtroom was abuzz as the anticipation built, and the onlookers stared at the man who made it snow. Carter Diamond was the head of "The Cartel," an infamous crime organization, and the entire city of Miami knew it. Scattered throughout the courtroom, the entire Cartel was in attendance, all of them wearing black attire.

With a model's posture, he sat next to his defense lawyer, slowly rubbing his salt-and-pepper goatee, thinking about the weight of the verdict. Accused of racketeering and using his multimillion-dollar real estate company to launder drug money, Carter could potentially go to jail for the rest of his life. And the case had drawn a lot of heat when key witnesses began to come up missing or dead, including a politician who turned informant to save his own behind.

A slight grin spread across Carter's face as he looked at the judge and realized that the chances of a guilty verdict were between slim and next to none. Just the night before, his accountant had wired the judge one million dollars to an offshore account. And just to ensure his freedom, eight of the twelve jurors had family members missing and in the custody of Carter's henchmen. At forty-three years old he was on top of the world. Fuck the mayor, Carter ran the city.

Carter glanced back at his family, his beautiful wife, daughter, and twin sons, who sat in the front row behind him. He winked at them and gave them his perfect smile.

It amazed Carter's family that he could be in the scariest of situations and still manage to make everything seem all right.

He stared into his wife's green eyes and admired her long, flowing, jet-black hair. Baby hair rested perfectly on her edges as her natural mocha skin glowed. Taryn, his wife, was a full-blooded Dominican and could have easily been mistaken for a top model. At age 38, she was just as beautiful as when she'd met Carter at 16.

Carter then glanced over to his daughter, Breeze, the spitting image of her mother and also his baby girl. At age nineteen, she was beautiful, intelligent, and being mixed with Black and Dominican gave her a goddess look. She had long, thick hair with green eyes, which made her every man's desire and every woman's envy. She smiled at her father, letting him know she was there to support him.

Carter looked at his two sons, Mecca and Monroe, AKA Money. They were the two oldest at twenty-one, and although they were twins, they were completely opposite. Mecca was the wilder of the two. He wore long braids and was a shade darker than Money. His body had twenty tattoos on it, including the two on his neck, enhancing his thuggish appearance. He was the more ruthless one. Mecca, wanting so badly to follow in the footsteps of his father and become the next kingpin of Miami, was notorious throughout Dade County for his trigger-happy ways.

Money was the humbler and more reserved of the two. His Dominican features seemed to shine through more than his twin brother's. His light skin and curly hair made him look more like a pretty boy than a gangster, but his looks were deceiving. Unlike his brother, he wore a neat low-cut and had no tattoos. Focusing more on the money aspect of the game, Money was a born hustler, and if the streets gave out degrees he would've had a doctorate. And although he wasn't as coldhearted as his brother, he wasn't to be underestimated.

It was in their blood to be gangsters. In the early eighties their Dominican grandfather ran the most lucrative drug cartel Miami had ever seen, and their father was his predecessor. Their family was "street royalty" by all means.

The media had a field day with this trial, covering it since day one. And CNN news cameras and several other stations had been broadcasting live footage of the spectacle for the last six months.

The sound of the gavel striking the sounding block echoed throughout the packed courtroom when the jurors filed into the courtroom after two hours of deliberation. The time had finally come for the verdict.

"Order in the court!" The judge looked over to the jury pool. "Has the jury come to a verdict?"

All eyes were on the juror as he paused before delivering the verdict, and all of the news cameras were pointed to Carter, trying to capture his reaction to his fate. The courtroom got so silent, you could hear a pin drop.

The head juror stood up with a small piece of paper in his hand. "Yes, Your Honor, we have. We the jury find Carter Diamond not guilty on all charges."

As the courtroom erupted with a mixture of victorious cheers and disappointing sighs, Carter nonchalantly loosened his tie and winked at the judge just before he firmly shook his lawyer's hand.

"Congratulations, Carter," the lawyer said as he gathered his files and placed them into his briefcase, the flashes from the cameras flickering nonstop.

"Thank you." Carter turned around to celebrate with his family.

When Taryn ran to him with open arms, he smoothly spun her around and kissed her passionately as if they were the only two in the room. He looked in her eyes and whispered, "I love you."

"I love you too, Carter Diamond," she replied as she hung from his neck.

Carter focused his attention on his kids. He kissed Breeze on the cheek, and she whispered in his ear, "Diamonds are forever."

"That's right, baby girl." Carter embraced her with one hand and grabbed Mecca's head with the other. He kissed him on top of the head and then did the same to Monroe.

Carter looked at all the reporters and photographers flocking in his direction and said, "Let's get out of here." With his wife and daughter under his arms, and his family around him, he made his way out of the courtroom.

News reporters tried to get a comment from him, but members of The Cartel stopped them before they could get close.

As soon as Carter exited the building, he embraced his right-hand man, Archie Pollard, AKA Polo, who was waiting outside of the courtroom, along with a wave of thugs wearing all black.

Polo leaned close to Carter's ear and whispered, "We did it, baby!"

"No doubt," Carter said. "This city is mine."

Carter stood at the top of the steps, feeling on top of the world. He pulled out a Cuban cigar and lit it, his diamond cufflinks blinging as he gave the world a view of his exclusive accessories. Looking out onto the streets, he noticed that the cops had sealed off the area to maintain traffic control. Everyone in the city was trying to get a glimpse of the "king of Miami."

Money noticed something wasn't right. As he looked at each officer and saw that they all had one thing in common. They all seemed to be of Haitian descent. By the time he realized what was happening, it was too late. One of the fake news reporters pulled out his 9 mm and pointed it at Breeze.

"Noooo!" Money screamed as he tried to warn his sister.

Polo became aware of what was about to happen and shoved the Haitian, causing him to tumble down the stairs before he could let off a shot.

All of a sudden, two dreadlocked Haitians popped out of the oversized dumpster, both with AR-15 assault rifles, and began letting off shots at The Cartel. It was complete pandemonium as shots rang out, hitting innocent by-standers, all in an effort to take out Carter Diamond.

Outnumbered, the members of The Cartel were defenseless. And Carter and his family were moving targets. As everyone scrambled for cover, Carter grabbed his daughter and wife and threw them to the ground, shielding them with his body.

A bullet ripped through Money's arm, and he fell to the ground. Mecca ran to his side, trying to protect his twin brother.

Meanwhile, Polo had pulled out his 9 mm and began to return fire. He had managed to keep the Haitians off long enough for the rest of The Cartel to come and help.

As the two crews traded bullets, many people got caught in the crossfire. The scene was a total bloodbath, with dead bodies sprawled out across the steps of the courthouse.

Carter, totally disregarding his own safety, tried his best to cover his two favorite girls from the raining bullets.

The police officer who had escorted Carter out of the courtroom shot at the Haitians. "Come on! Follow me," he yelled. He looked at Carter and waved his hand, signaling them to follow him.

Carter hated police, but at that moment he was happy to see one. He gathered up Taryn and Breeze and followed the officer back into the courthouse.

"I parked my police car in the back. Come on! They'll be coming in here after you any second now," the cop said as he closed the courthouse door.

"Let's go, y'all," Carter yelled in a panicked voice to his wife and daughter as they followed the policeman down the stairs and into the basement.

Carter thought about his sons outside, but he knew they could hold their own. His main concern was the women. They raced through the court halls and finally made it to the exit. Just as the cop said, he had his squad car parked in the back. Carter felt relieved. They all got in, and he frantically searched his wife's and daughter's body, making sure they were okay. "Are you hit? Are you guys okay?" he asked as he continued to search their bloodstained clothes. He realized that the blood was not from them, but from all the blood flying from the other people.

"No, I'm good, Poppa," Breeze answered, tears flowing down her face, her hands shaking uncontrollably.

"I'm okay," Taryn said.

Carter hugged and kissed them both and thanked God that they were okay. His concern now was for his sons. He looked up at the cop that sat in the front seat and said, "Thanks, bruh. Look, I need you to take them to safety while I go back and—"

Boom!

Before Carter could finish his sentence, the cop put a hollow-tip through his head, his blood and brains instantly splattering all over his wife's and daughter's face as he stared with dead eyes.

In total shock, both of the women yelled, "Noooo!"

The cop pulled off his hat, and his short dreadlocks fell loosely. He pointed the gun at Carter's body and filled him with four more bullets, ensuring that the job was done. The screams of the women didn't seem to bother him as he smiled through the whole process. The man wasn't a cop at all, but a full-blooded Haitian that could pass for a regular joe, his light skin disguising his heritage.

He pointed his gun at Taryn, and she looked directly in his eyes, unafraid of death, while Breeze gripped her father and cried hysterically. The Haitian couldn't bring himself to pull the trigger and hopped out the car.

This was the beginning of a war.

Welcome to The Cartel . . . first of a trilogy.

Chapter One

"Girl, females are going to hate, regardless. That's how
you know you're *that* bitch."
—Taryn Diamond

Seven Years Earlier

Carter sat at the head of the table with both of his
hands folded into each other. He briefly stared at each of
his ten head henchmen in the face as he looked around
the table, then to his right-hand man Polo, who sat to
his right. As he always did, Carter took his time before
speaking. He always chose his words carefully and spoke
very slowly with his deep baritone voice. He poured Dom
into his oversized wine cup and took a sip.

"Family, today The Cartel has expanded. The days of
hand-over-fist pay is over. It's a new day, a new world, a
new era. For the last ten years I have flooded the streets
of Miami with the finest coke and built a monopoly. I
love all of you as if you were my own blood. That's why
I'm giving you the opportunity to grow. You can't hustle
forever. I've recently acquired a real estate company, and
this way we can turn all of this dirty money into clean
money. I want all my niggas to eat with me. So, if you
want to be a part of this, here is your chance." Carter took
another sip and passed the cup to Polo.

Without saying a word, Polo took a sip out of the same
cup, signaling his response to Carter's proposition. He

passed the cup to the next man, and he did the same. Real niggas did real things, and the cup got passed around the room, and all men drank from the same cup.

Mecca and Money peeked around the corner, listening in on their father's meeting. Although they were only fourteen, they wanted so bad to be a part of The Cartel. They both noticed at an early age how much respect their father received from everyone in the streets. They would get special treatment in school from teachers and students. Some of their friends' parents would go as far as giving them presents and hinting to them to mention it to their father. They loved how real their father was. He would talk to bums on the street as if they were the president of the U.S.A. He treated every man as his equal, as long as they respected him and his family. For lack of better words, Carter was a real nigga, and both of the twins admired him greatly and wanted to be just like him . . . but for different reasons.

Monroe loved the way his father stayed fresh at all times and was a great business and family man. He observed his father's style and immediately idolized him. Carter never wore the same shirt twice and only wore the finest threads. Money also took note of and admired his father's business savvy. Every move he made was a business move, a move that would benefit him in the future.

Mecca, on the other hand, admired his father's street fame. He loved the way the street respected and feared his father. He would hear stories about his father being the man that made it snow, in a city that had never seen a winter season, or cutting off fingers if workers stole. In Mecca's eyes, Scarface didn't have shit on his father.

While other kids were worried about candy and chasing skirts, Mecca was thinking about chasing money and being the next king of Miami.

As they eavesdropped on the conference, they watched as each man took a sip out of the cup.

"Mecca and Money, come in here." Carter calmly grabbed the cup that had rotated back to him.

Since Carter's back was toward them, when he called their name, it surprised them. It was as if he had eyes in the back of his head. They slowly walked into the room. The boys stood nervously next to him, knowing that they got caught spying on him and that their father was very strict when it came to handling business. They eased up when they saw a slight grin form on his face.

Carter passed Money the cup and looked around to make sure their mother wasn't around. "Take a sip of that," he said.

Money looked at the cup as if he was scared to take a sip.

Mecca noticed his brother's uneasiness and grabbed the cup from him. He took a gigantic gulp of the liquor, and a burning sensation rushed down his throat. It took all of his willpower not to spit it out. His face twisted up as he put one hand on his chest, hoping that the burn would go away.

Polo noticed his expression and laughed loudly. "That'll put some hair on ya chest, nephew!" he said in between laughs.

Carter joined him in laughter as he watched his other son take the cup and take a moderate sip. Money's face didn't change its expression. He took the gulp like a man.

Money handed the cup back to his father and stood there with his chest out, as if he was trying to prove that he was a man. Mecca followed suit.

"Why were you two eavesdropping on Poppa?" Carter playfully hit both of his sons in the chest.

Money shrugged his shoulders as if to say, "I don't know."

Mecca looked around the table, seeing nothing but hustlers and killers. He then looked at his father, who sat at the forefront of them, and a smile spread across his face. "Poppa, I want to be just like you. I wanna be a gangster," Mecca said as he stepped in front of his brother.

One of the hustlers at the table chuckled as he looked at Mecca. "Li'l man got hustle in him. That's a gangster in the making right there," the man said.

Carter shot a look at the man that said a thousand words. If looks could kill, the man would've been circled in chalk. "No, my son will never be that. Watch ya mouth, fam," Carter stated firmly as he focused his attention back on Mecca. "Look, sons, you are better than this. This game chose us, we didn't choose the game. You got the game twisted. I do this, so you don't have to," Carter said, as a somber feeling came over him. It hurt his heart to hear Mecca say that he wanted to be a gangster like him.

"Let me show you two something," Carter said before he looked at his henchmen that sat at the long red oak table. "How many of you have lost someone close to you because of this drug game?

Slowly everyone at the table raised their hands, to help Carter prove a point.

"How many of you go to bed with a pistol under your pillow?" Carter asked. "And how many of you want to get out of the game?"

Mecca and Money looked at everyone in the room holding up their hands, and Carter's point was proven.

"Do you two understand, this game . . . is not a game?"

Mecca and Money nodded their heads, understanding the lesson that their father had just sprinkled them with.

"Take another sip of this and head to bed." Carter smiled and handed Money the cup. After the boys took a small sip of the drink, he grabbed both of their heads at the same time and kissed them on top of it. "Don't tell your mother," he whispered to them just before they exited the conference room.

Although Carter had explained to them the cons of the street life, the allure of the game was too powerful, and Mecca and Money wanted in. They just had to wait their turn.

Breeze stood at her balcony, totally astounded by the view, and stared into the stars. Her balcony hovered over their small lake and faced their gigantic backyard. The Diamond residence was immaculate. They had just moved there, and it was a big jump from the dilapidated projects of Dade County. Breeze's 12-year-old eyes were lost in the stars as her mother stood behind her and brushed her long hair. This was a ritual they did every night, and Taryn used this time to bond with her daughter.

"Breeze, what's wrong, baby? Lately you haven't been saying much," Taryn said as she continued to stroke her daughter's hair.

Breeze took her time before she spoke. Her father had taught her to always think about what to say before saying it. "I just miss back home. I don't like it out here. None of my friends are out here. I hate it in South Beach, Mommy." Breeze's eyes got teary.

"I know it's hard to cope with the sudden change, Breeze, but your father is a very important man, and it wasn't safe for us to stay in Dade. He did what was best for the family," Taryn answered, knowing exactly how Breeze felt. She herself had been a daughter of a kingpin, so she knew what it was like to be sheltered because of a father's notoriety.

"I just don't get it. Everybody loved Poppa in the old neighborhood. Why would we have to move?"

When it came to his baby girl, Carter held back nothing. He answered any question she asked him truthfully,
wanting to give her the game, so another boy couldn't
game her. She knew her father was a drug dealer, but in
her eyes he was the greatest man to walk the earth. She
saw how he treated her mother with respect at all times.
She witnessed him put his family before himself countless times and admired that. She wanted her husband to
be just like her daddy.

"I know exactly how you feel. You're too young to
understand right now, Breeze. Just be grateful that you
have all of this. Most women will go through their whole
life and never have the things you already have."

*I understand. I know what's going on. I know Daddy
is the dopeman. I know more than you think I know.*
Breeze went into her room and flopped down on her can-
opy-style bed. Tears rolled down her cheek as she curled
up on her pillow. She missed her old home so badly. She
just wanted to be a regular around-the-way girl.

Taryn, her white silk Dolce and Gabbana nightgown
dragging on the floor as she went to her daughter's side,
slowly entered the room and saw that the sudden change
really was bothering her only daughter. She sat on the
bed and began to rub Breeze's back. "I know exactly how
you feel, Breeze. My father too was an important man. I
remember when I was your age and was going through
the same dilemma. My father, your grandfather, was
an important man also. I had it much worse. It took
the murder of your uncle for my father to move out the
hood. Your father is just being cautious. If anything ever
happened to you or your brothers, our hearts would
break. He's just protecting you." Taryn reminisced about
her deceased brother, who died when she was only ten.
He was only 15 years old when he was kidnapped and
killed while her father was in a drug war.

"I know that we have to live like this, but it's just not fair. I feel like I don't belong here. All the girls at school look at me funny because I'm mixed, and they whisper bad things about me. I try to ignore them, but it still hurts my feelings."

"Girl, females are going to hate, regardless. That's how you know you're *that* bitch." Taryn smiled and squinted her nose.

Breeze couldn't help smiling at her mother's comment. She looked at how beautiful her mother was, and her comment made her look at things differently. *Maybe they do look at me enviously*, she thought.

Before Breeze could say anything in response, Carter cleared his throat, startling them. He looked at how gorgeous the two main women in his life were. He suavely leaned against the doorway with his arms folded. "What are you guys smiling at?" He walked toward them.

"Nothing, baby." Taryn smiled and winked at Breeze. "Just girl stuff."

Carter bent over and kissed Taryn and then kissed Breeze on top of the head.

Taryn knew that Carter had come to tuck Breeze in, as he did every night, and decided to leave them alone. "I'll be in bed," she whispered to him. "Goodnight, baby," she said to Breeze as she tapped her leg. "I love you."

"I love you too, Mommy."

Taryn strolled out of the room, her stilettos clicking against the marble floor as she made her way out. Taryn would never get caught without her heels on. Nightgown and all, she always looked the part, playing her role as the queen of her husband's empire. She was wifey, there was no doubt about that.

Carter stared at his wife as she walked away and then turned his attention back to Breeze. "Hey, baby girl." He sat next to her.

"Hey, Poppa." Breeze sat up and focused on her father.

"How was school today?" Carter asked as he rubbed her hair.

"It was okay, I guess."

"Breeze, you know I know when you're lying. Tell Poppa what's going on."

"I just miss my friends. The people at my school are so funny-acting. I wish we could move back home." Breeze dropped her head.

Carter placed his finger under her chin and slowly raised her head. He looked into his daughter's green eyes and smiled. "Baby girl, don't worry about that. Everything takes time. They will come around eventually. I tell you what"—Carter stood up and smoothly put his hands in his $400 Armani slacks—"Why don't you call up some of your friends and tell them you're having a sleepover. You can invite as many of them as you want. I'll have a limo pick up each girl. Would you like that?"

Breeze eyes lit up, and she gave him the biggest smile ever. "Yes! Thank you, Poppa," she said as she leapt into her arms.

Carter had promised himself that he wouldn't let outsiders enter his new home, but he had a weak spot for Breeze. She was his only daughter, and he spoiled her more than he did his twin boys.

"What about boys?" Breeze looked at her father. "Can I invite them too?"

His smile quickly turned into a frown as he looked at Breeze like she was insane.

"Gotcha!" she said as she broke out into laughter.

"Baby, don't do that," he said, joining her in laughter. "You almost gave this old man a heart attack." Although Breeze was joking around, he knew that the day when she would be serious was soon to come. A day that he would dread.

Chapter Two

"There is strength in numbers, and we will get through
this as a family."
—Polo

Polo took a deep breath as he pulled into the South
Beach, one of the many suburbs of Miami. As he looked
around at the perfectly landscaped lawns and the children playing carelessly in the streets, he realized why
Carter had moved his family so far away from the hood.
With its gated community and million-dollar structures,
it seemed as if it were a million miles away from the grit
of the ghetto. Carter, positive that the upscale environment of South Beach would protect his household from
the harsh reality that the street life had to offer, had told
him that the move would be good for his family, but he
was wrong. Now Polo was forced to bury his man.

Polo and Carter had known each other since they were
young and hardheaded coming up in the trenches of
Dade County. They quickly formed a brotherly bond as
they took over the streets and inevitably entered the drug
game. *The Cartel* was what they were labeled, a notorious, criminal-minded organization that was willing to
stay on top by any means necessary. Carter and Polo had
put in work for many years and worked hard to surround
themselves with thoroughbreds that respected the hustle
of the streets as much as they did. They earned money,
power, and respect.

That is, until the Haitians from Little Haiti discovered the money that was being made and tried to muscle them out of town.

Carter's demise proved to Polo that the Haitians weren't to be taken lightly. He just hated that it took the death of their leader to figure that out. Nobody was untouchable. Now he had a nagging pain in his heart, and the stress of retaliation on his brain, but he knew that his hurt didn't compare to that of Carter's family.

When he pulled into the driveway to the ten-room, 7,000 square foot home, he prepared himself for the heartache that he was about to encounter. Polo personally made sure that Carter's wife and children were taken care of. He knew that they would be okay financially, but he was determined to ensure their safety. No expense was spared when it came to the security of their family. There were about ten armed henchmen stationed outside of the house, and he acknowledged them with a nod as he passed by and walked into the Diamond home.

"Unc Po." Mecca slapped hands with his father's best friend.

Polo could tell that Carter's death was weighing heavily on his heart by the sad look in Mecca's eyes. Polo then turned to Monroe and pulled him near as well. He held them close, his arms wrapped around their shoulders. All three men had their heads down.

Polo told them, "I know it doesn't feel like it right now, but it's gon' be all right, you hear me?"

Tears formed in Money's eyes. He nodded his head, praying that his Uncle Polo was right.

Polo whispered in their ears, "You both have to be strong for your mother and Breeze. This is gon' hit them the hardest. You know how protective your father was of them. It's time to step up to the plate, twins. You got to pull your family back together."

Both boys nodded in agreement as they quickly wiped the tears from the eyes. Having been trained by their father to never show emotion, they knew that to cry was to show weakness,

"Where are your mother and sister?"

"They're still upstairs," Money stated.

Polo ascended the steps two at a time. He approached the bodyguard that he had hired to stand by Taryn's side. "Fuck you doing?" he whispered harshly.

The bodyguard quickly snapped his cell phone shut, but before he could put it safely in his pocket, Polo slapped it out of his hands.

"Do I fucking pay you to talk on your cell phone?" Polo pointed his finger in the man's face. It didn't matter that he was only five foot eight, and that the bodyguard was 270 pounds of pure muscle. "How the fuck you supposed to protect anybody when you're focused on your fuckin' phone? As a matter of fact, get your ass out of here. Put somebody on this job that want to make this money, you pussy!"

The man didn't even protest as Polo lifted his Steve Madden and kicked him in the ass toward the staircase. He looked over the landing and yelled, "Mecca, show that mu'fucka the door and bring one of them niggas up that take this shit seriously." Polo fixed his clothes and wiped himself down before he knocked lightly on Taryn's door.

"Come in," she called out. "It's open."

Taryn looked as beautiful as ever standing in front of the full-length mirror in her white-on-white Dolce suit that fit nicely around her slim frame, the skirt stopping directly below her knee and hugging her womanly shape. Her neck was framed with rare black pearls that matched the pearl set that clung to her ears. Her long, layered hair was pulled back into a sophisticated bun. She spared herself of applying makeup because she knew that eventually her tears would ruin it anyway. Her natural beauty was enough to take Ms. America's crown, and her Dominican features made her look more like a mature model than a mother of three.

"Taryn, it's time to go," Polo stated as he stood in her doorway.

She nodded her head and closed her eyes as she said a silent prayer to God. *Please give me the strength to get through this for my children. They are all that I have left. Take my husband into grace and take care of him until we meet again.* "Okay, let's go," she said, trying to hide the shakiness in her voice.

She walked out of the room and down the hallway to her daughter's room. "Breeze," she said as she opened the door. "It's time."

"I don't think that I can do this," Breeze stated, tears running down her cheeks. It was obvious that she had been crying for hours, because her eyes were red and swollen. The distress from her father's murder was written all over her young face. It was almost as if her legs gave out from underneath her, because she fell onto the bed and put her head in her hands.

Taryn and Polo rushed to her side. Polo knew that Breeze would take her father's death the hardest. His only daughter, she was his pride and joy, and he had treated her like a princess since the day she was born. Breeze could do no wrong in his eyes, and they had shared a special connection all her life.

"I can't believe he's gone," Breeze stated. She felt as if the life was being squeezed out of her. "I can't do this, Uncle Po." She dreaded putting her father to rest. Never in her nineteen years had she felt a pain so great.

Taryn embraced her daughter as they sat side by side, cheek to cheek. "I know that you can't do this, but *we* can," she stated. "There is strength in numbers, and we will get through this as a family."

Polo was speechless as Taryn's words moved him. It was then that he realized that Carter was truly a lucky man to have a woman such as her by his side. He left the room and descended the steps. He waited in the foyer with Mecca and Monroe, and when the two women came down the steps, they all walked out of the house together.

The limo ride was silent as each member of the family tried to wrap their minds around the death of their patriarch. He was the one who protected them, fed them, clothed them, loved them, made all of their decisions. He was their educator and best friend, so without him, they all felt lost.

Dear Carter,

I know that you do not know me, but I know you very well. You are my husband's son. I have thought about you countless times. If you are anything like your father, I can picture your dark chocolate skin, strong jawbone, and wide, soul-searching eyes. I wish that I could have written you under better circumstances, but I am not contacting you to deliver good news. My husband, your father, has left this earth. He was killed, and although you do not know him, I wanted to give you the chance to say your goodbyes. His funeral will be held Saturday June third, 2008. I hope that you will join us in celebrating his life. Everyone is expected to dress in white attire. He would not want us to mourn his death, but to come together as a family and appreciate his life. I know that is how he would have wanted to go out.

Sincerely, Taryn Diamond

Carter folded the letter up and put it in the pocket of his Armani suit jacket. He had received the letter a week ago and was debating whether or not he should actually go to his father's funeral. He had never known his father, never even heard his voice.

Why am I here? he thought in confusion as he looked at his reflection in the mirror. His designer suit was tailored specifically to his six-foot frame, and his broad, strong shoulders held the material nicely. A small gold chain hung around his neck, displaying a small gold cross.

Checking his watch, he realized that he didn't have much time to get to the church. He reached underneath the hotel bed and pulled out a duffle bag that contained pure white cocaine and two handguns. He figured he may as well drop off some dope to some of his people in Atlanta while in the Dirty South. That way, if the funeral ended up being a waste of time, he wouldn't have wasted time and money coming to town.

He pulled out his chrome .45 and tucked it in his waist. He rubbed the waves on his freshly cut Caesar and took a deep breath. He had to prepare himself for what he was about to do. He had felt resentment toward his father ever since he was a young boy. He had never understood why he had grown up never knowing the man that helped create him. Although he harbored these feelings, he still felt obligated to show his respects.

A nervous energy filled his body as he headed for the door. It was time for him to say goodbye to a man he'd never met.

As the bulletproof limousine pulled up to the church, Carter's henchmen walked up and surrounded the vehicle.

"Leave your guns in the car," Polo instructed Money and Mecca. He opened the door and prepared to step out.

Mecca told him, "The heater staying on my hip, Unc. Them dreadhead mu'fuckas deaded my father. I'll be damned if they do the same thing to me." He popped the clip into the chamber.

"First, I'ma tell you to respect your mother, and watch your mu'fuckin' mouth, Mecca."

"Nah, Mecca's right, Uncle Po," Money said. "We need to be strapped at all times."

Polo put his foot back into the car and closed the door so that their conversation wouldn't be heard. "Okay, listen"—He looked around at the shaken Diamond family—"I know this is hard for you, but you have to trust me. Your father was like a brother to me. I love this family as if it is my own. I would never let anything happen to anyone of you. Now I promised the pastor that I wouldn't bring any weapons into his church. Your father's funeral is neither the time nor place for them. Everyone inside of that church is here to show love."

Mecca and Money reluctantly pulled their guns out of their pants and sat them on the seat in the limo.

"Everything will be fine," Polo assured them. He stepped out of the car first and held out his hand for Taryn, who graciously accepted. He put his hand on the small of her back and led her through the crowd of onlookers, and her children followed closely behind. They were all surrounded by so many bodyguards, one would have thought that Barack Obama was entering the building.

White on top of white was the only thing that could be seen when entering the sanctuary. Everyone attending the funeral was clad in their best white suits, and there were white bouquets of lilies and hydrangea flowers scattered throughout the room. The turnout was unbelievable.

Taryn immediately halted her footsteps when she saw the titanium and black casket that sat at the front of the church. She looked around the room and observed the extravagant funeral that she had put together, making sure to take care of each arrangement personally. No one knew her husband the way that she did, and she wanted to make sure that his funeral was comparable to none. Carter Diamond was the best at everything he ever attempted, so Taryn made sure that he went out in style.

She slowly walked down the aisle. The closer she got to her husband's casket, the weaker her knees became, but she had to be strong. She couldn't let the world see her break. *My children are depending on me,* she thought.

When she finally reached the casket, her heart broke into pieces at the sight of her lifeless soul mate lying before her. She reached down, grabbed his hand, and kissed his cheek. She whispered, "I will always love you, Carter, always." She then turned with the poise of royalty and took her position on the front pew as the first lady of the streets.

Mecca's heart beat wildly in his chest. He had never imagined what he would do if something ever happened to his father. He prided himself on being strong and fearless, but there was no way that he could be strong now. And the sudden loss of Carter made him fear death.

He stepped down the aisle and gripped the sides of his father's casket when he saw his ashen face. The glow that his dark skin had once possessed was gone, and his eyes were sunk in. He felt the swell of water in his eyes cloud his vision. He closed his eyes to hinder them from falling. He picked the tiny cross necklace off his chest and kissed it. It was the chain that Carter had given all of his children the day that he'd brought them home from the hospital: fourteen-karat gold crosses to hang around their necks. The chain had been changed over the years, but the cross was still the original. The children all valued their chains with their lives. Mecca walked over to his mother and sat beside her, trying to keep his emotions at bay.

Monroe stepped toward the casket next. He thought of all the times his father had spent with him. He knew that he needed to absorb all of Carter that he could, because this was the last time that he would ever see him again. He gripped his father's hand and leaned in close to his ear, as if he could still hear him, and said, "Thank you for everything, Poppa. I'll remember everything that you taught me. I'll never forget you." With those words, Money joined his brother and mother.

Breeze graced the church aisle as if it were a runway. All eyes were on her as she paused midstep. She knew that her life had been changed forever. Her Poppa, comparable to none, was the man of her dreams, and she didn't want to let him go. She stepped up to the casket as she fought to keep her pain under control. But as soon as she touched his cold skin, she lost it. Against her will, a small cry escaped her lips, and a fountain of tears cascaded down her precious face. She leaned over her father, gripping his hand, and silently prayed for God to take care of his soul. The sight of her so broken-down caused the attendees to break down as well. Her collapse signaled the collapse of the entire church, and wailing could be heard throughout.

Mecca went to her side, to get her to let go of Carter's hand. "Come on, *B*." He gently rubbed her hair and lifted her head. "Don't hold your head down. Poppa wouldn't have that." He smiled at her gorgeous face, and she gave him a weak nod of agreement as she finally left her father's casket and sat with the rest of her family.

Just as the pastor took his place at the podium, the church doors clanged open. Gasps rang out throughout the church as all eyes focused on the young man who stood in the doorway. Speculative whispers traveled throughout the pews as everyone watched the young man walk down the aisle. From his skin tone, to his confident stride and striking features, he was identical to the man they were there to bury, and one would be able to guess without reading the tattooed name on his neck that he was Carter Diamond's son. It was almost unnatural the resemblance that the two shared.

Mecca's eyes followed the man as he approached the front of the church. "Fuck is that?" he hissed.

"The nigga looks just like Poppa," Money commented in amazement.

"Mommy?" Breeze looked at her mother.

But Taryn needed no explanation. She knew exactly who the young man was. He was Carter Jones, her husband's illegitimate son.

Polo leaned into her and whispered, "Taryn, I have something to tell you. Carter didn't mean to—"

Without taking her eyes off the young man, she said, "Don't worry about it, Polo. No need for you to explain. I know who he is."

Carter felt the questioning glares of the people surrounding him. He stopped in the middle of the church and stared at the casket up front. His heartbeat was so rapid that he felt sick to his stomach. *I shouldn't be here,* he thought.

Just as he turned to leave, four men with long dreadlocks entered the room. They were the only ones wearing black. Carter frowned at their blatant disrespect. They bumped him violently as they walked past, but Carter let it ride as he turned his head and watched them continue down the aisle.

Mecca's temper immediately flared. He reached in his waistline for a pistol that wasn't there. "Fuck!" he whispered as he began to stand.

Polo grabbed his arm to halt him. "Wait a minute," he stated. "This is a part of the game." Polo didn't expect the Haitians to make their presence felt at the funeral. He had underestimated their coldness.

The church was silent as everyone waited to see how things would play out. It was no secret that the Haitians were responsible for Carter's death. The dreadheads walked up to the casket and stood silently with their heads down, as if they were in prayer.

Taryn gripped her sons' hands and let out a sigh of relief.

"See," Polo said, "they're only here to represent the Haitians. They're just showing respect for the deceased. We gon' handle that, just not here."

Before the words could reach Taryn's ears, she was in an uproar as she watched the Haitians hawk up huge gobs of spit and release them on her husband's body, defiling Carter's corpse.

"Hawk ... twah!"

"Hawk ... twah!"

Breeze watched in disbelief as the Haitians raised their feet and forcefully kicked the casket off the table, causing the body to roll out onto the floor. Carter's head hit the floor hard, causing a loud crack to pierce the air, and the attendees gasped in horror.

Polo, Mecca, and Monroe sprung into action, with the rest of The Cartel behind them.

"Poppa!" Breeze shouted as she rushed toward the front of the church to retrieve her father's corpse from the floor.

Taryn yelled in alarm, "Breeze!" as she watched her daughter head toward the mayhem.

Suddenly, bullets from an AK echoed throughout the church, *Tat, tat, tat, tat, tat, tat!,* little flashes of fire kissing the air, and was followed by the sound of people screaming and running for the exit.

Breeze didn't care about the gunfire. She just wanted to get to her father. But before she could reach him, one of the Haitian gunmen snatched her up.

Taryn yelled, "Breeze!"

Carter looked in horror at the front of the church. He recognized the young girl from pictures that he had been sent when he was younger. *She's my sister,* he thought as he pulled out his .45 without hesitation.

He stood up and scrambled to get between the screaming people as he aimed his gun and released one shot. His bullet hit its intended target, and the man holding Breeze dropped instantly.

Carter's clip was quickly emptied as the gun battle continued. He was clearly outnumbered, but that didn't stop him from reaching in his ankle holster and pulling out his 9 mm pistol as the three remaining Haitians shot recklessly, clearing a path to leave the church. Using his natural instinct for survival, he picked up the body of the dead Haitian and wrapped his arm around his neck, putting him in a chokehold from behind. The deadweight was heavy, but it was the only way for him to shield his body from the bullets being sent his way.

Carter yelled, "Y'all niggas wanna clap?" and shot his nine with one hand, while moving toward the Haitians, who were now headed for the door.

Carter's gun spit hollow-points toward the Haitians as the dead body in front of him absorbed his enemy's fire. *Pow! Pow!*

Just as he reached the exit door, one of the Haitians yelled, "Me going to kill you, muthafucka!" And the three remaining Haitians made a run for it.

Carter continued to shoot until he was sure they left the building. Once he was positive that everyone was safe, he dropped the dead Haitian to the floor and let off his last round into his skull. "Bitch nigga!" He hawked up a huge glob and spat directly in the dead man's face, returning the favor on behalf of his dead father.

He rushed over to Breeze's side. Rocking back and forth, she was holding on to her father's dead body and crying hysterically.

"Are you okay?" he asked.

"Get the fuck away from her. We don't know you, mu'fucka!" Mecca stated harshly as he pulled Breeze off the ground. Her head fell into his chest as he walked her away.

Polo looked around at the carnage inside of the sanctuary. A couple people had been injured, and the church was destroyed. "We've got to get the fuck out of here," Polo stated. "How did they get in?" Polo yelled in anger. He patted the Young Carter on the back. "Come on, let's go before the police show. Follow me back to your father's house."

A look of surprise crossed Carter's face.

"Yeah, I know you're his son, but right now that's the least of my worries. Just follow me back to the house. We need to talk." With those words, Polo escorted the family out of the church, and they darted inside of the limo.

The Haitians had sent a clear message—They were out for blood, and they weren't going to stop until The Cartel was out of commission.

Chapter Three

"Brother or not, next time homeboy step to me like that,
I'ma rock his ass to sleep."
　　—Young Carter

The Diamond family sat in their living room along with
Polo and Young Carter. The room was quiet; no one knew
what to say. Taryn's and Breeze's eyes were puffy because
of all the crying they had been doing, the horrific images
of their loved one being kicked out of his casket haunting
their thoughts.

Mecca's Armani shoes thumped the marble floor as he
paced the room back and forth, totally enraged, two twin
Desert Eagle handguns in his hands. The Haitians had
shown the ultimate sign of disrespect and were sending
a clear message that they were trying to take over Miami.
In fact, it was Carter's decision to not cut the Haitians in
on his operation that ultimately led to his assassination.

Polo stood up and slowly walked to the window. He
looked in the front and saw henchmen, all strapped, scattered around the house to ensure their safety. With the
Haitians merciless tactics, he didn't underestimate them.
He saw the fire in Mecca's eyes and tried to calm him.

"We have to keep our heads on straight. These niggas
are going hard at us. The Cartel still runs Miami, remember that! We have to retaliate to get our backs out of the
corner." Polo removed the suit jacket that rested on his
black silk shirt.

"Fuck that! Let's get at they ass, guns blazin'! I don't give a fuck no more!" Mecca screamed, a single tear sliding down his cheek.

Money stared into space without blinking. He was in complete shock. The death of his father was very hard on him. He remained silent as his twin brother let out his frustrations. He couldn't come to grips with his father's death.

Money snapped out of his daze and looked over at Young Carter. It was obvious that he was his brother. He looked so much like Carter, it was unbelievable. Young Carter had thick, dark eyebrows just like his father, and he even shared his tall, lean frame. His mannerisms were even the same. He watched as Young Carter rested his index finger on his temple while in deep thought, just as his father used to do.

It hurt his heart that his father had an illegitimate child. The perfect image that he had of his father was somewhat tarnished by the news. *How could this nigga be my brother? Daddy wouldn't step out on Momma like that,* Money thought as he stared at Young Carter.

Taryn noticed Money staring and decided to address the issue. She knew that there were other things to worry about and wanted to explain the complex situation. With tears still streaming down her face, she stood up. "I want you guys to meet Carter Jones . . . your brother." Taryn rested her hand on Young Carter's shoulder.

Breeze lifted her head in confusion. She looked at her mother and then to Young Carter. "What?" she managed to murmur. She couldn't believe what her mother was telling them. The words were like daggers to her heart. She was so busy grieving, she didn't even notice how closely Young Carter resembled her Poppa.

As she looked at Young Carter, she couldn't believe her eyes. She just thought that he was one of The Cartel's henchmen. He looked like a younger version of her father. *Oh my God*, she thought as she placed her hand over her mouth.

Mecca came closer to Young Carter and stared him in the face while saying harshly, "This ain't my fuckin' brother. He ain't a mu'fuckin' Diamond!" Mecca gripped his pistols tighter, refusing to believe the obvious.

Young Carter returned the cold stare at Mecca, not backing down whatsoever, but he still remained silent. Young Carter was respectful because he was aware that his presence presented a conflict to the Diamond family, but he wasn't about to back down from anyone. And the way Mecca was gripping his pistols caused Young Carter's street senses to kick in. He slowly slid his hand to his waist, where his own banger rested. He stood up so that Mecca wouldn't be standing over him. Young Carter was a bit taller than Mecca, so he looked down on him, not saying a word.

"Mecca, he is your brother! Sit down and let me explain," Taryn yelled, trying to reason. She rushed over to Mecca as the two men stared at each other intensely. "Mecca!"

"Fall back, bro," Money said as he stood up.

Mecca jumped at Young Carter as if he was about to hit him, but Young Carter didn't budge. Not even a blink. Young Carter grinned, knowing that Mecca was trying to size him up.

"That's enough!" Polo made his way over to them.

Young Carter kissed Taryn on the cheek and whispered, "Sorry if I caused any more heartache. I didn't come here for this." And before Taryn could even respond, he was headed for the door.

"Yo, wait!" Polo said as he followed Young Carter out.

"Let that bitch-ass nigga go!" Mecca yelled as he continued to pace the room.

It took all of Young Carter's willpower not to get at Mecca, but he figured that he would give him a pass for now.

Polo caught up to Young Carter just before he exited the house. "Yo, youngblood, hold up a minute."

"There's no need for me to be here. I don't know why I even came to this mu'fucka anyway," Young Carter stated, an incredulous look on his face.

"Listen"—Polo placed his hand on Carter's shoulder, trying to convince him to stay—"Mecca has a lot on his mind right now. The family really needs you."

"Look, fam, I ain't got shit to do with them. I just came to pay my respects and keep it pushing, nah mean? Brother or not, next time homeboy step to me like that, I'ma rock his ass to sleep." Carter clenched his jaw.

Polo took a deep breath and saw that Carter was no-ticeably infuriated, but kept his composure out of respect. Young Carter reminded Polo of his late best friend in so many ways. Polo looked into Carter's eyes and said, "Just give me a minute to talk to—"

Carter cut him off mid-sentence, not wanting to hear any more. "Look, I'll be at the Marriott off South Beach until tomorrow night." With that, he left Polo standing there alone.

Chapter Four

"They were willing to murk women, children, hustlers,
the good, the bad, and the ugly. It didn't matter, anybody could get it, if the price was right."
—Unknown

Carter flipped through the different denominations of
bills as he diligently counted the cash that he had just acquired from his flip. After the drama he had experienced
during his father's funeral, the business he handled in
Atlanta made the trip better for him. He would now leave
the Dirty South $180,000 richer. *This was definitely
worth the trip,* he thought to himself as he admired the
hood riches that lay scattered across the hotel bed.

He put the bills in ten-thousand-dollar stacks and
wrapped rubber bands around each one, to keep the
money organized. He counted the cash a second time
to verify that his money was on point. He was thorough
when it came to his paper. It was the one thing that he
knew he could depend on. Money was his first and only
love. Getting money came first in any situation, and he
was determined to keep his pockets fed.

A knock at the door interrupted his thought process,
and out of habit, he grabbed his pistol from the night-
stand and approached the door.

He had been a bit paranoid from the events that had
taken place the day before at the funeral, so he wanted to
be as cautious as possible while he was in Miami. A nigga
would never catch him slipping.

He looked through the peephole and eased up when he noticed the distorted image of his father's right-hand man. Sliding the chain from the hotel door, he unlocked it and allowed Polo to enter the room.

Polo shook his head as he looked at Young Carter. It was still hard for him to get over the resemblance. Young Carter looked so much like his father, it was uncanny. It was a shame that the two men never got the chance to know one another. "Can we talk?" Polo asked, both hands tucked inside of his pants pockets.

"Yeah. come on in." Carter set his pistol down. "You want a drink?"

Polo stepped inside. "Nah, I'm good." He noticed how on point Carter was and thought to himself, *like father, like son.*

Carter walked over to his bed and pulled the bedspread over the stacks of money to conceal his business. He then sat down and motioned for Polo to take a seat in the chair across from him.

"I just came to see how long you were in town for?" Polo knew that the Diamond family needed Young Carter now more than ever.

"I'm ghost tomorrow. Ain't nothing here for me."

Polo had predicted this reaction from Young Carter. He didn't expect him to feel any sense of responsibility to his family at first, but he knew that if he could convince Carter to stay around long enough, the attachment would eventually grow.

"I know this is a lot to put on your heart right now, but your family needs you."

Carter was quick in his response. "They don't even know me," he stated with disdain. "That's not my fam. I've only known one woman my whole life, and she the only family I need, nah mean?"

"Nah, I don't know what you mean, Young Carter. I saw the look in your eyes today when that Haitian mu'fucka had your baby sister at gunpoint. Only a man who had love in his heart would get at them niggas the way you did. It was instinct for you to protect her. Whether you want to admit it or not, that is your family, and they need you, especially Breeze."

"Ain't nobody tried to protect me my entire life. I've been out for self from the time I was old enough to understand the rules of the game. I don't have time to baby-sit. That's not my responsibility." Carter wanted to make it clear that he wasn't trying to get to know the Diamond family, didn't want to be around them.

Seeing their expensive house and luxury vehicles just made him resent his father even more. While he grew up in Flint, Michigan, a city that was known as the murder capital, the man that made him was taking care of the family that he had abandoned his first-born for. The pain of growing up without a father had left a bad taste in his mouth.

Polo stood and shook his head from side to side. "Everything isn't always as it seems, Young Carter. Your father had his reasons for leaving you and your mother, and it wasn't because he didn't love you."

"It really doesn't matter now. That man is in the ground, and it doesn't affect me. I just came to pay my respects. I didn't come here for nothing more or nothing less. That man has never done a damn thing for me, so I'm not gon' even hold you up and say that I feel obligated to step up and take care of his family. A better man might be able to, but that's not me."

"I understand you are frustrated Young Carter. You come here and see how happy your siblings are, and you feel cheated. I know you're asking yourself why you didn't have the same upbringing, but believe me, your father did the best he could under the circumstances," Polo stated, defending his best friend.

When Carter didn't reply he continued, "Your father—"

"I don't have a father. The nigga got my mother pregnant and then left us for dead to come play house with another bitch."

"Look, you need to watch your mouth." Polo, enraged by Young Carter's blasphemous statements, had to set the record straight. "I can't just sit here and allow you to disrespect my man like that. You don't know shit about nothing. If it wasn't for your father, you and your mother would have been dead a long time ago. He had to leave you in order to protect you."

"Fuck is you talking about?" Carter asked, hostility and anger in his tone.

Polo could see that the young man's temper was beginning to flare and then remembered that Young Carter had a valid reason to be upset. He took a deep breath and calmed himself down, to de-escalate the situation. "Look, Young Carter, I'm not here to bump heads with you. As your father's best friend, I've got nothing but respect for you. You have a misconception about the man that your pops was. I'm not saying that every decision he made regarding you and your mother was right, but he did the best that he could. Think about it, young'un. Your mother worked as a CNA since you were young. She's bringing home thirty stacks a year at the most, but you grew up in a two-hundred-thousand-dollar house in the suburbs of Flint. Who do you think purchased that house? Who paid those bills? Use your head, young fella. How many fourteen-year-old boys you know kept a thousand dollars a week in his pocket? When you graduated you were pushing a limited edition Mercedes. Who do you think copped that car for you? Let me tell you, it wasn't Mommy."

Polo's words were enough to silence Carter and make him think. His mother never told him about his father. She had never even talked about him and would explain their living situation by saying that she worked overtime, sometimes double-time, to allow them to live the way that they did. She often claimed to hit big at the casino or to have the winning lotto number. She had given her son every excuse in the book to explain the extra income. *All this time my father was sending money back home to take care of me?* Carter tried to wrap his mind around the fact that his father had never forgotten him.

"Your father never missed a beat in your life, son. You may not have gotten the chance to meet him, but he knew everything about you. It was nothing for him to fly in and out of Flint in the same day just so he could be at your Friday night football games. Remember that game you ran three hundred yards against Southwestern?"

Carter nodded his head as he placed it in his hands. "Yeah, I remember."

"Your father was there. I know he was there because he dragged my black ass with him every week. Every touchdown, every awards assembly, your graduation, he was there for all of that. When you got into that trouble with the law as a juvenile, he made sure that the case was thrown out. Fifty grand made that little mishap disappear from your record.

"Your father loved you very much, but he was a hustler too. He met your mother when she was fifteen and he was seventeen. They dated throughout his senior year in high school, and when it was time for him to go to college, he regretfully left her to better himself. Your mother was so upset with him that when he moved down here she stopped contacting him. He tried to call her, but she would never return his calls. A couple years later he met Taryn. She was beautiful, unlike any woman he had ever

met, and they fell in love quickly. She is a full-blooded
Dominican though, and they don't play that interracial
dating shit. He had to prove himself time and time again
just to be with her. If it weren't for his persistence and
her refusal to leave him alone, they never would have
been allowed to stay together. He knew that she was the
daughter of Emilio Estes."

Carter lifted his head in surprise at the notorious drug
lord's name. His eyebrows rose in speculation as he
thought, *I know this nigga ain't talking bout—*

Before Carter could finish his thought, Polo said,
"Yeah, I'm talking about *the* Emilio Estes."

"Damn!"

"Emilio took Carter under his wing. His coke connect
allowed Carter to establish The Cartel as the most notorious and prosperous illegal enterprise Miami has ever
seen. Emilio was clear in his concerns though. He told
Carter that if he wanted to be with his daughter then he
would have to keep up the lifestyle that she was accus-
tomed to. Emilio told him that his family had to come
first and that if he ever disgraced his daughter in any way
then it would be the death of him."

"So he deserted me and my moms. He chose his family
in Miami over me."

"Your father didn't even know about you until you were
a young child. Your mother didn't even tell him that
she was pregnant. When he found out, Taryn was pregnant with the twins, and if Emilio ever found out, you
and your mother would have been put in direct danger.
Knowing that he could trust his wife, he told her about
you and your mother. Although she was upset at first, he
explained that he had never cheated on her. She agreed
to never tell her father, and they sent your mother money
to support you from that day forth. It pained him that
he couldn't get to know you. He wanted to be a part of

your life, but his connections with the Dominican Mafia prevented that from happening. You are his first-born. You look just like him. He loved you wholeheartedly."

Confusion and anger took over Carter's body. He didn't know if he should be relieved or enraged. "It still doesn't make up for the years I spent never knowing him. I don't give a fuck what I'm facing. When I have a shorty, my seed gon' know who I am. I'm gon' be a man and take care of my family, no matter what the circumstances are. Money can't make up for the times he wasn't there. My mother couldn't teach me how to be a man. I turned to the streets for guidance. My father came to my games, but he wasn't the one who showed me how to throw the football. He never showed me how to grip a pistol. He ain't show me shit. I had to learn all that shit off humbug on my own."

"Sending you money and supporting you from afar was the only thing he could do. That cash kept you fed and a roof over your head. Your mother didn't have to worry about shit. She chose to never spend the money on herself. She never had to work another day of her life if she didn't want to. He made sure of that." Polo looked in Young Carter's eyes, trying to read him.

Carter stood up to signal that he was done with the conversation. "It still doesn't matter. This ain't home, and first thing tomorrow I'm out."

Polo stood as well, He shook his head in contempt. "A'ight, I hear you, but now you hear me. There's a war going on. Your little brothers and your baby sister need you right now. They weren't raised the way you were. They're spoiled, and they underestimate the seriousness of what's going on. This family needs your leadership, your protection. There's a lot of unfinished business that needs to be handled. Your father's seat at The Cartel is waiting to be filled."

Carter's silence was enough to let Polo know that he was considering his options. He headed for the door. Before he left the room, he said, "There's a meeting tomorrow night at the Diamond house. Your presence should be felt. If you're still in town, you should drop in. I'll be in touch."

As the door closed behind him, Carter thought of all the times he had wondered about his father. He was going crazy as he tried to recount the endless gifts his mother had given when he was growing up. He remembered growing up in the inner city up until the age of ten. At that time, his mother had mysteriously packed up all their belongings and moved them to the suburbs of Grand Blanc. *That must be around the time that Carter found out about me,* he thought to himself.

A part of him wanted to leave town and never look back, but another part of him wanted to stay. The part that had seen the beautiful face of his baby sister, the part that had witnessed the arrogant swagger of his brother Mecca, and calculating discreetness of his brother Monroe. His emotions were at an all-time high, and for the first time in his life, he was indecisive.

Unable to stay cooped up in the hotel suite, he grabbed two stacks of money and headed for the door. He needed to clear his head. He figured that the best way to do that was to visit the floating casino that sat at the end of the pier on South Beach. He didn't know that gambling ran through his veins like blood. It was a habit his father also had. What he did know was that it relaxed him, which was just what he needed at the moment.

Carter stood at a lively crap table with nothing but hundred-dollar chips in his rack. The casino was unusually packed for a Sunday night, and every table was crowded with eager participants just waiting to be taken by the house. Carter was lax from the top-shelf Rémy he was sipping on. The liquor and the intense thrill of the game had calmed him down since his earlier encounter with Polo.

"All bets set!" the dice handler yelled before maneuvering the ivory across the table and placing them in front of Young Carter. "Dice out!"

With his drink still in one hand, Carter picked up the dice with the other and tossed them toward the other end of the table with a nonchalant swagger. The dice tickled the fabric as they danced before finally landing.

"Yo! Eleven, yo!" the dealer shouted, indicating that eleven had landed on the face of the dice.

Uproarious celebration erupted around the table as everyone collected their wins and anxiously awaited Carter's next roll. He had been on a hot streak all night, hitting point after point. His luck was unbelievable. He had held the dice for forty-five minutes, which was almost impossible to do in the game of craps. He schooled the dice against the table with his head down as he watched his hands work their magic. He concentrated heavily on his technique. Every hustler had his own rhythm with the dice, and Carter was no exception.

"Excuse me, can I get in here?"

Hearing the feminine voice amongst the crowd of boisterous men caused Carter to look up. A brown-skinned girl with shoulder-length, almond-colored layers and hazel eyes squeezed into the empty rack next to him. She was so close to him that her sweet perfume played games with his senses, and he felt his manhood acknowledge her presence. He put the dice down as he watched her reach into her skintight Seven jeans and pull out a small wad of money. He waited for her to throw her cash on the table before he continued his roll.

The dealer handed her a hundred dollars worth of chips, and she put them in her rack, arranging them by denomination. He smirked at her as she made a pattern with the different color chips. It was rare that he saw a woman at the crap tables, and the one beside him had his full attention.

The men around the table grew impatient, some of them clearing their throats to signal to Carter that he should pick up the dice.

The young woman squirmed beside Carter, trying to find her place between the big men surrounding her.

"My fault, baby," Carter stated. "Here, let's do it like this." He turned sideways and allowed her to ease in comfortably at the table, giving her more room to play.

"It's all right. You good," she responded with a New York accent that immediately told him that she wasn't from Miami. She looked up at him and smiled as he stared down onto her five foot five frame.

Captivated by her presence, he made mental notes as he admired her wide hips, thin waist, and perfectly manicured fingers and toes. His intense focus on her caused her to blush.

She lay her chips on the table. "Can I get a seventy-two dollar six?"

Carter noticed the small tattoo on the back side of her wrist that read Murder Mama. That immediately piqued his interest. She then pointed to the dice, reminding Carter that it was his roll. Carter tossed the dice at the end of the table. "Here go your six, ma."

"Hard six!" the dealer yelled.

The girl jumped up and down and squealed with joy as if she had just won a million dollars, and Carter couldn't help but chuckle at her enthusiasm.

The man next to her was so in awe of the woman that he dropped her a twenty-five-dollar chip and winked at her, saying, "Lady luck!"

The man was so busy taking a peek at Miamor's ass that he didn't notice her lift three of his five-hundred-dollar chips out of his rack. Miamor bent over and pretended to fix the strap on her stiletto, giving the man a nice view of her assets. She did all of this in less than ten seconds. While everyone was busy collecting their money from the dealers, Miamor used the distraction to her advantage. When she stood, she gave the old man a half-smile that seemed to light up the room.

Carter shook his head with a smirk on his face as he watched the young woman's game.

"What's so funny?" she asked with laughter in her voice as she looked up at him, one hand plastered to her hip, the other reaching onto the table to collect her cash.

"Nothing, ma. I'm just happy you won." Carter licked his full lips.

"Okay," she stated playfully, as she discreetly scanning his body from head to toe. "I see you clowning me, but you need to be minding your own business and hit that six again. I still got money on the table. Everybody ain't balling like you. I see you betting with your purple chips," she said, referring to his full rack of big bills.

"I got you," he said as he prepared for his next roll. "What you drinking on, ma?"

"Hpnotiq and Goose," she replied.

The two of them stayed at the crap tables all night. They joked and laughed, flirting openly with each other. Young Carter enjoyed her company and appreciated her presence because she took his mind off his deceased father. He noticed the size of her pockets as she tried to keep up with his bets and had calculated that she had lost at least two grand trying to hang in the game.

As the crowd began to disperse, they eventually were the only two left at the table. Drunk and feeling good, they made dumb bets, Carter not caring how much he spent, but the young lady watching every dollar that the dealers trapped up.

"Seven out!" the dealer called. The enthusiasm had left his voice, and it was apparent that everyone at the table was exhausted.

"Looks like your luck has run out." The girl leaned against the table. She faced him, her head cocked to the side, her eyes low and sexy from the effects of the liquor.

"I guess so," he replied as he stepped to her, closing the space between them. "You all right. You look a little tipsy."

The girl smiled seductively and answered, "Just a little bit, but I'm good. I didn't come here alone. My girls are around here somewhere. This was fun. Thanks for the drinks."

As she began to walk away, Carter gently grabbed her forearm. "Aye, hold up," he stated softly. He reached into his Prada pockets and pulled out a wad of money. He peeled off twenty hundred-dollar bills and opened the girl's hand to put them inside.

"What are you doing?" Her eyes opened wide in surprise. "I can't take this."

"Whenever you're in my presence, everything's on me. That should make up for what you lost, even though it wasn't yours to begin with." He rubbed her hand before letting it go.

"A'ight, I see you," she replied with a laugh. She threw the money onto the dice table.

"What you doing, ma?"

She put her hands to her lips as if to shush him and then told the dealers to put it all in the field. She picked up the dice, tossed them down the table.

"Two field bet two !" the dealer yelled in excitement, amazed at the young woman's luck. "Double the payout."

Carter shook his head in disbelief. He couldn't believe that the girl had just put two stacks on such a dumb bet. The payout was lovely.

She picked up six thousand dollars from the table and handed him back three thousand. "I make my own ends, but it's nice to know that there are gentlemen still out here."

Before she could walk away, Carter said to her, "I didn't get your name, shorty."

She brought her lips close to his ear. "That's because I didn't give it to you. If you're worth getting to know me, I'll see you again," she replied with a smile as she walked away from him.

"Miamor, who da fuck is da fine-ass nigga you were kicking game to?" Aries asked as she sat in the backseat of the Honda Civic.

"Aries, shut up. Wasn't nobody kicking game to nobody. I wasn't worried about that nigga. Y'all bitches just don't know how to tail a mu'fucka without being all obvious. Our mark was at the crap table in the upstairs VIP. I just chose the table that gave me a nice view to the stairway, so I'd know who was coming and going. Dude was just a prop to make it realistic. My eye never left the prize," Miamor replied, making sure that she kept her eye on the all-black Lamborghini that was three car lengths in front of her.

"I don't know, Mia. It looked to me like you were check-ing for him," Robyn teased.

Miamor smacked her lips, and a guilty smile spread across her face.

"Bitch, me knew it!" Aries shouted excitedly in her Barbadian accent.

"A'ight, a'ight, I'll admit it. The nigga was a little fly. He had an A game on him. But why the fuck is we discussing that nigga? This ain't playtime. Let's get focused on this business," Miamor stated, trying to get back to the task at hand.

"Now da bitch wanna be focused," Aries stated smartly.

"I know, right?" Robyn burst into laughter.

To the average person, the three girls were rare beauties out for a night on the town. One would have never guessed that these contract killers—They called themselves "the Murder Mamas"—were responsible for sixty percent of the drug-related murders in the Dade County area. If the paper was right, they were down for the job. Nobody was an exception. They were willing to murk women, children, hustlers, the good, the bad, and the ugly. It didn't matter, anybody could get it, if the price was right.

Come on, Mia, keep up with this fucking car, Anisa thought frantically as she watched her sister's car disappear in the side mirror. Her heart began to beat rapidly as she began to think of a way to buy her friends time to catch up.

"Mecca, can we stop at this gas station up here?" she said in her sweetest tone. "All those Long Islands are making me want to pee." She rubbed her left hand on his crotch.

Mecca's dick immediately responded to her touch and began to stiffen as he looked at her fat ass, which was melting into his leather seats. "Nah, we almost there. Just hold that shit. Come put those pretty lips to work," he said with a tone of authority that didn't leave her room to object.

Anisa looked in her mirror once again. *Fuck! Mia, where are you?* She unbuckled her seatbelt and leaned into Mecca's lap. She unzipped his pants and pulled out his throbbing dick. She was immediately aroused by the sight of his long thickness, which was a shade darker than his light skin, and was the prettiest thing she'd ever seen. Her mouth watered in anticipation. The fresh smell of Sean John cologne greeted her nostrils, and she licked her lips in delight. Anisa loved a big, clean dick and figured, since she was about to kill the nigga, she might as well give him the best head job of his life before sending him to meet his Maker.

She licked the head of his length and circled her tongue seductively around his hat, and his manhood jumped from excitement.

"Ohh shit," he uttered as he kept one hand on the steering wheel and put the other on the back of her head. He entangled his fingers in her hair and gently pushed her down onto him.

Anisa took all of him into her mouth, gagging a little from his size. Her mouth was wet and warm, and Mecca was in heaven as he glanced down at the beautiful woman. She slobbered on his dick as she deep-throated him. She knew she was nice with her tongue.

Not even five minutes had passed, and she felt the swell of his rod as he neared ejaculation. He closed his eyes and almost forgot he was driving as she slid her mouth down one last time, tickling the vein underneath his shaft on her way up. It was a wrap, as she sat up and watched Mecca come into an orgasm.

"Damn, baby, let's get you up to this room. A nigga need some of that." Mecca slipped one of his fingers up her skirt, pushing her thong to the side, and massaged her swollen clit.

"Hmm," Anisa moaned as Mecca fingered her dripping pussy. He was working his fingers in and out of her like a dick, and she began to work her hips as she felt the pressure building between her legs. *If this nigga can work his fingers like this, I know he can fuck good. I might have to fuck his sexy ass before I kill him.*

Anisa squirmed in her seat and continued to check her mirrors as she enjoyed the pleasure that Mecca was providing her.

Mecca pulled into the parking lot of the Holiday Inn and hopped out of the car, leaving his car with the valet. He pulled out a hundred-dollar bill and gave it to the valet. "Take care of my car," he said. "You fuck that up, I fuck you up. Understand?"

"Yes, sir," the valet answered immediately.

Mecca walked over to the passenger side and opened the door for Anisa.

"Thanks," she stated with a smile. She grabbed his hand and walked beside him.

When they entered the hotel, Mecca checked into a regular room, using one of his many aliases.

Butterflies circled in Anisa's stomach because she was sure that her girls had gotten lost in the sauce of Miami's nightlife traffic. *It doesn't even matter because, once I slip this nigga this GHB pill, this mu'fucka gon' be out for the count anyway. It'll give me enough time to let them know where I'm at,* she thought as she reluctantly followed Mecca up to the tenth floor of the hotel.

"Where in the hell did they go?" Robyn asked in a panicked tone. "I don't see them! Can you see the car?"

"Nah, but you need to chill out. Now is not the time to start tripping. We've done this shit a thousand times. Let's just stick to the plan. Anisa knows how to handle herself. We fucked up by losing her, but she'll contact us when she can," Miamor stated confidently.

"Me don't know, Miamor. This job is on a whole 'nother level. What if she needs us?" Aries asked.

Miamor could feel the fear creeping into her team's heart. She knew that fear could easily manipulate any situation, and she was fighting to keep control. *Where are you, Nis? Let me know something,* she thought, as she too began to worry. She didn't like the fact that she had lost their mark, but she knew Anisa would be able to handle herself until they could get there.

"I just need to use the restroom. I'll be right out," Anisa said as she entered the hotel room. She quickly disappeared behind the safety of the bathroom door and locked it behind her. She sat on the toilet, her heart beating a mile a minute and pulled out her two-way. She sent the text to her crew—*I'm at the Holiday Inn on Biscayne Blvd. Room 1128*—then quickly put her phone in her purse and flushed the toilet for show. She washed her hands and walked out of the bathroom.

As soon as she opened the door, Mecca was standing there looking her in the face.

"Oh!" she exclaimed as she dropped her Chanel clutch purse onto the floor. "Shit!" she yelled out. The contents of her purse spilled out onto the floor, and she quickly squatted to retrieve the tiny packet of white powder before Mecca could see it.

"Why you so jumpy, ma?" Mecca asked, his stare penetrating her, his hand caressing the side of her face. Then he looked into the bathroom suspiciously. "I need to get in there." He walked inside and closed the door behind him.

"O-okay."

Anisa rushed over to the mini-bar and set up two glasses. She used Grey Goose because she didn't want to use dark liquor, afraid that the residue from the drug might float to the top. She used her finger to mix the powder into the glass and then removed her silver Chanel dress. She stood in her black Victoria's Secret bra and thong, and her four-inch Chanel stilettos.

When Mecca walked out, he saw her standing with two drinks in her hand. He admired the curves of her body. Her wide hips, flat stomach, and apple-shaped bottom

gave him an instant hard-on. He could only imagine the
treasure that she had between her thighs, and couldn't
wait to taste her.

"Here, baby, I fixed us a drink. I want us to relax so that
we can enjoy the night."

"I'm not drinking tonight."

*Fuck you mean, you not drinking, nigga? You been
drinking all fuckin' night, and now you want to change
up?*

Mecca could see the distress on her face. "That's a
problem?"

"No, baby, I just want to make you feel good. How about
we order some room service, have some drinks, and
afterwards I'll let you put your dick in something warm?"
She put the glass of Grey Goose in his hands and left a
trail of kisses from his ear, to his chest, and continued to
move south. She got to his pants and unbuckled his belt.

Just as she was about to go to work, he grabbed her
hair forcefully, almost tearing it from the root. "You
drink it," he stated in a menacing tone.

The look in her eyes confirmed his suspicions. When
she didn't respond, he continued, "You got two choices.
You can either drink it, or I'm gon' blow a hole through
your top." He removed his gold-dipped Beretta 950
Jetfire and aimed it at her head.

"Mecca, what the hell is your problem?" Anisa stood to
her feet. "I just want to make you feel good. You're pointing guns in my face and shit. We're supposed to be having
a good time," she whined, trying to flip the situation in
her favor.

"Save that shit. You think I didn't see the car that was
following us, bitch? Drink up. If there's nothing going on,
then you have nothing to worry about."

Anisa realized her plan wasn't working. *Where are you,
Mia?* She slowly reached for the drugged drink. She knew

that if she drank the liquor, she would be committing suicide. Mecca had peeped her shade, so she knew that she had to act fast. She grabbed the drink from his hands and tilted it toward her mouth.

Mecca watched intently, but just as her lips touched the glass, she violently threw the liquor in his face and darted for the door.

"Bitch!" he yelled as he cleared the wetness from his face and chased after her. She managed to open it slightly, but he was right on her ass and slammed his weight against her, causing the door to slam shut. Then he grabbed her neck and tossed her to the floor as if she were the size of a rag doll.

"Aww!"

"Bitch, you trying to poison me? You trying to set me up?" Mecca aimed his gun at her head, and before she could deny his accusation, he silenced her with two to the dome.

"There that nigga go!" Robyn pointed to Mecca as he rushed out of the parking lot.

Mia peered into his car, and immediately noticed that he was alone. It was at that instant that she felt something was horribly wrong. "Where's Nisa?" she asked, her tires screeching as she pulled up swiftly to the valet curb. She hopped out of the car and shouted to the valet, "Leave my car running. I'll be right out!"

Robyn and Aries were right behind her. They didn't wait for the elevator to make it down to the hotel lobby and darted straight for the staircase. Each girl was silent, all fearing the worst.

When they finally made it to the eleventh floor, Miamor took off for Room 1128. They were all out of breath but kept running as if their lives depended on it.

Mia noticed that the room door wasn't closed completely and pushed it open forcefully. "Nisa?" she called as she saw her sister lying in a small pool of blood. Tears immediately came to her eyes.

"Oh my God!" Robyn shouted when she saw her good friend's body on the floor.

Aries was speechless as she watched Miamor kneel by her sister's side.

"No! Nisa, wake up, baby. Don't do this, Anisa. Get up!" Mia shook her big sister's body as if she were only asleep. "Come on, help me get her up!" she yelled, looking back at Aries and Robyn for help. "Come on! She needs to get to a hospital. Help me please," she cried, her voice sounding like that of a small child.

"We've got to get out of here," Robyn whispered as she kneeled down beside Miamor.

"No! I can't leave her. Nisa, come on, get up."

"Mia, there's nothing that we can do for her now. It's too late. She's gone," Robyn said sadly. "She's gone."

Miamor nodded, her face frowned up in pain. "I know," she whispered in between sobs. She leaned over her sister's dead body and whispered in her ear, "I love you, Nis, and I'm going to kill him, I promise." She kissed her sister's cheek and then exited the room.

At first, killing the Diamond family was something that she had been paid to do. Now it was personal, something that she had to do, and no matter how long it took her, she would have her revenge.

Chapter Five

A nigga move a brick, and think he Gotti o' somebody.
—Young Carter

The conference room in the Diamond house was in complete silence. Every hustler in the room felt awkward. It was the first time that The Cartel had held a meeting without their boss, Carter, and everyone seemed to be just staring at his empty head seat. Carter usually started the meetings with a statement or a quote, and with him not there, things were odd.

Polo noticed the uneasiness of the henchmen and stood up. He looked at Money and Mecca, who sat to the right of him, and then back at the henchmen. He took a deep breath as he unbuttoned his Armani blazer.

He walked behind Carter's former chair and rested his hands on the back. "Family, we have suffered a great loss, but business must go on. Carter would've wanted it that way. The Haitians, them mu'fuckas have no respect for the game. These niggas playin' fo' keeps, but we won't bow down to anybody, believe that. We have to let them know that The Cartel still runs Miami, point-blank!" Polo slammed his fist on the glossed oak table.

The occupants of the room included all of the head block lieutenants from each district of Miami. They all seemed to see their paper begin to decrease and knew exactly what the reason behind it was.

Polo looked at Money, who had a law notebook in front of him. "Money, how much did we bring in this week?"

Money ran his finger down the pad and uttered reluctantly, "Two hundred fifty-three thousand."

This only added to Polo's frustrations. "What the fuck is going on, fam? Our operation does a million easy. That's barely enough to pay the runners. What the fuck!" Polo said as he focused back on the henchmen.

One of the henchmen rubbed his hand over his face and goatee. "Man, most of my workers are quitting or siding with the Haitians. They got niggas shook. Ma'tee and his crew are trying to take over the city."

"Got niggas shook? Fuck outta here. Y'all need to recruit more thoroughbreds then, real talk! We have to let the Haitians know that just because Carter is gone, it doesn't mean we're layin' down. We have to get back at them."

"That's all I been trying to hear." Mecca pulled out his twin pistols and laid them on the table. "And you know what? Them mu'fuckas tried to send some bitch at me the other day, like I wouldn't peep the shit."

"What happened?" Polo asked.

"What you mean, what happened? I left that bitch stankin' in the room." Mecca nonchalantly looked around the table.

"I told you about fuckin' with them hoodrats, Mecca. We in a war right now! You can't do that, bruh. You could have got yoself killed," Money said, obvious aggravation in his tone.

"Bitch ain't gon' catch Mecca slippin', believe that! I knew what the bitch was on from the jump. I just wanted to get the pussy before I off'd her ass." Mecca leaned back in his chair.

The henchmen laughed at how cold Mecca's attitude was.

Polo and Money were the only ones not amused by his overconfidence. They knew how wild and careless Mecca could be. They also knew eventually his rashness, if not controlled, would lead to their downfall.

Before Polo or Money could respond, the room grew quiet. Everyone's eyes shot to the door. Some of the henchmen thought they were seeing a ghost, but it wasn't a ghost. It was Young Carter.

Polo turned around to see Young Carter standing there with an all-black hoody, and a diamond cross that hung down to his belt buckle. Polo smiled, knowing that his talk with him paid off.

Mecca sucked his teeth, letting it be known he wasn't comfortable with Young Carter's presence.

Polo waved his hand over the table. "Come in and join us."

Young Carter scanned the room slowly and looked at each man present. He then walked over to the table full of hustlers.

"Everyone, this is Carter . . . Young Carter," Polo said, introducing him.

Everyone greeted him with a simple head nod or a "What up," and Carter returned the greeting with a nod.

Money pulled the chair out that was next to him. "Have a seat."

Carter accepted the gesture and took a seat.

Young Carter and Mecca traded mean stares as he walked over to the chair, but both of them knew that it couldn't escalate, seeing they were blood brothers.

Polo cleared his throat and picked up where he left off.

Carter peeped the surroundings and realized that his father was a powerful man. The man he went his entire life hating had boss status, the same thing he was trying to achieve. He looked at the henchmen and noticed that all of them wore luxury, expensive threads and didn't look like the hustlers he was used to back home. Miami had a whole different vibe.

Young Carter stuck out like a sore thumb amongst the others. Carter was from the street, he was hood, and he couldn't help it, so he wore street clothes, knowing nothing better. While he wore Sean Jean and Timberland, the men were rocking Roberto Cavalli and Ferragamo suede shoes, and everyone wore black.

He chuckled to himself. *These niggas really believe they on some Mafia shit, fo' real. Fuck outta here. A nigga move a brick, and think he Gotti o' somebody.* He couldn't understand why they had formed this organization. Where he was from, hustlers didn't come together at any point. It was a dog-eat-dog mentality, and everyone was out for self.

In the game since he was sixteen, Young Carter began moving bricks by age twenty-one. He was what you call a bona fide hustler. His mother died when he was twenty, and after that, he didn't look back. He went hard on the streets. He had Flint, Michigan's coke game on lock.

Now, at the age of twenty-five he ran the city, hooking up with a coke connect from Atlanta and completely taking over. Young Carter didn't know it, but he was following in the footsteps of his father.

He focused his attention on what was being said in the meeting.

"We have to get at the Haitians somehow. We have to be strategic," Polo said as he sat down and began to rub his hands together. He was in deep contemplation, and for the first time, he felt the burden of not having Carter's strategic mind. Times like these, Carter was a genius at playing mental chess with the enemies.

In the middle of the discussion, Money's cell phone rang. Normally he wouldn't pick up his phone in the middle of a meeting, but he had been waiting on that particular call. He flipped open his cell. "Yo," he said in his low, raspy tone.

He remained silent for a minute, while getting the information from the other end of the phone. Then he closed the phone without saying a word.

"One of my sources thinks he knows where Ma'tee resides," Money stated, referring to the leader of the Haitian crew that had them under fire. "Maybe we need to pay him a visit."

Oversized Chloe glasses covering her eyes and Foxy Brown pumping out of the speakers, Miamor cruised down the interstate pushing 100 mph in her rented GS coupe, her long hair blowing in the wind along with the chronic weed smoke she blew out. She could afford to buy her own car, but in her profession she had to switch up whips like she did panties, to be less noticeable. She took another long drag of the kush-filled blunt and inhaled it deeply.

Throughout the last two years, her and her crew put . . . their . . . murder . . . game. . . . down. I mean, you couldn't mention *Murder Mamas*, if *homicide* wasn't in the sentence. Murder for hire was the best way to sum it up. She had done numerous hits for Ma'tee; none of them resulted in these extreme measures. The recent loss of her older sister had Miamor's mind churning. She wanted to get revenge on the man that killed her blood. But first, she needed to see Ma'tee to get more information on this guy. Only thing she knew about him was that his name was Mecca and that Ma'tee had beef with his family. When they took a job, they usually didn't ask a lot of questions. The only question they needed answered was how much money was involved.

"I swear, that nigga is dead, word to my mutha," Miamor said to herself in her strong New York accent. She pulled off the freeway and entered the town of Little Haiti, where Ma'tee lived.

After taking several back streets and dirt roads, she made it to Ma'tee's residence. Miamor looked at the elegant mansion and the 15-foot steel gate that was the entryway. She pulled the luxury car up and stuck her hand out of the window to push the intercom button. A video surveillance camera faced directly toward her from the gate.

"Wan, state cha name?" a voice sounded in a Haitian accent.

Miamor yelled loud enough so she could be heard, "Yo, it's Mia!"

"Who?"

"Miamor, mu'fucka! Open up!" she spat out of frustration.

A brief moment of silence came about just before the sound of the metal clanked, opening up for her. Miamor maneuvered the vehicle through the gate onto the long driveway leading up to the palace. She noticed that Haitians were scattered throughout the property, all holding assault rifles.

It was only the second time she had been there, but the view amazed her once again. The grass was perfectly even and greener than fresh broccoli. The driveway was filled with luxury cars and lined with beautiful flowers.

As she got closer to the front of the house, she noticed that a birthday party was going on. It was about fifty children in the front yard with noise-makers and birthday cake on their faces and hands. She saw all of the children gathered around watching the clowns making balloon animals, the kids screaming loud in excitement, and all of them having a ball.

A beautiful dark-skinned girl with long, kinky hair was front and center. She had on a princess crown and was happily being entertained by the clown as she instructed him on what balloon animal to make.

That must be Ma'tee's daughter, Miamor thought, immediately noticing the resemblance. She felt bad for intruding on an obvious family event, but she needed to speak with Ma'tee. She also saw a couple of grown women amongst the crowd, obviously the mothers of some of the children. She thought about returning another day, but she had to find out more about Mecca. She was itching to slice his throat. It was only a matter of time.

Miamor made her way to the front door, where two dreadlocked men stood guard. "I'm here to see Ma'tee," she stated as she stood before them.

Without saying a word, the guards, both with pistol in hand, stepped aside and opened the door for her.

Miamor stepped in and admired the crystal chandelier that hung from the cathedral ceiling. The glass wraparound stairs stood in the middle of the room and sat on white marble floors. The all white walls and furniture gave the home an immaculate look. Miamor headed to the back for the sliding glass door.

Another man stood in front of it with a pistol in his holster. Unlike the other men, he didn't wear dreads; he had a neat low cut, but was darker than all of the other guards.

Miamor looked past him, trying to spot his boss. "Where can I find Ma'tee?"

"I need to check you before you approach Ma'tee," he said, shifting his stance.

"I left the guns in the car," Miamor shot at him.

"Sorry, ma. I still have to search you." He shrugged his shoulders and crossed his arms.

Miamor let out a loud sigh, letting him know that she was irritated. She held out her hands and spread her legs. Her Seven skinny jeans hugged her large behind. Her stiletto heels made her assets seem even more enticing as she remained bent down and he began to search her from feet on up.

He felt her tiny ankles in search for a gun hostler.

"You know I can't fit a damn pistol in these tight-ass jeans."

"You never know," he said, continuing to feel her upper leg. He paused, his nose level with her crotch.

"Smells good, don't it?" Miamor said, hip to his game.

"Yeah, smells very good actually." He looked up at her and gave her a perfect smile.

"Too bad you'll never see her. I wouldn't even let you taste it. Hurry up. I ain't got all day." Miamor turned her eyes to the ceiling. She didn't even give him the respect of looking at him.

The man was obviously embarrassed as he hurried up and finished searching her. Once he was done, he opened the sliding door and pointed her toward Ma'tee, who was laid out in front of the pool, accompanied by beautiful women. There were beautiful women swimming completely nude in the pool while a shirtless Ma'tee watched in enjoyment as he sat on a beach chair, his feet crossed, and his hands behind his head. His dark skin glistened in the sun, and his muscular abs seemed to poke out of his stomach.

As Miamor slowly walked over to him, the clicking of her heels against the ground gained his attention.

He slowly sat up and looked at Miamor, admiring her shape and oversized behind. He loved the way her jeans hugged her hips, and the way she switched them when she walked. Her thighs seemed to stick out more than her waist. Ma'tee's fantasies were short-lived as he realized that Miamor was more than just a stunning woman—She was a cold-hearted killer too.

His dreads were much neater than his henchmen's, and the tips were bleached brown. He shook his head, letting them fall freely from its original ponytail. "Hello, Miamor," he said, greeting her with a smile.

"Hi, Ma'tee," she answered as she took a seat next to him. "Sorry I interrupted your daughter's birthday party, but I really needed to talk to you."

"Ey, mon, no problem. Miamor me girl, ya know," he said as he put on his shirt.

"Yeah, I know. But, listen, I need to know more about this nigga Mecca." Miamor stared in Ma'tee's eyes with deep sincerity.

Ma'tee saw the desperation in her eyes and stood up. "Why don't chu come to me office. We talk 'bout it."

Miamor nodded her head and got up to follow Ma'tee.

Just as they were about to reach the glass door, Ma'tee's daughter came running out. "Dadda, Dadda, the clown made me a giraffe, see?" She handed him the balloon animal.

"Yes, me see me baby girl's giraffe. Wonderful!" Ma'tee scooped her up in his arms.

"Dadda, when are you coming out to play with me?"

"Dadda gots to talk to me friend Miamor. Then me come back to you, okay," he said before he kissed her on the cheek.

"Okay. I have to use the bathroom now," his daughter said as she wiggled down and ran towards the wrap-around stairs.

Ma'tee stared at his only child and smiled. He looked back at Miamor and said, "That's me baby girl, right dere."

Miamor smiled and continued to follow Ma'tee into his back office. She walked into the office, where Ma'tee had shelves of books. In fact with his extensive collection, the office sort of looked like a library. His shiny red oak table sat in the middle with a deluxe leather chair behind it.

Ma'tee made his way over to the chair and sat down. He waved his hand to the seat in front of him. "Sit, sit."

Miamor accepted his offer and sat down.

Ma'tee continued, "Me sorry to hear 'bout your sista.
Me never meant for dat to happen, you know."

"Yeah, I know." Miamor dropped her head.

"Look, me still pay you, okay." Ma'tee pulled a briefcase
from under his desk.

Miamor looked at the briefcase as Ma'tee popped it
open. It was fifty stacks, ten percent of the agreed amount
that they were to be paid after the job was completed.
She knew that they didn't deserve the money, because
they didn't finish the job, so she declined.

"No, Ma'tee, I'm good. I just want to know how to get at
the mu'fucka that killed my—"

A loud scream came from upstairs. "Aghhh!" It was the
voice of a little girl.

What the fuck? Miamor turned around and looked
toward the door.

Ma'tee instantly recognized the voice to be his daughter's and grabbed his gun from his drawer and hurried to
her aid.

Armed Haitians rushed upstairs where the girl was and
what they saw devastated them. There were five bodies
lying in their own blood, and Ma'tee's young daughter
stood in the middle of them. She had discovered them
when she went to use the restroom. The dead bodies
were scattered throughout the hallway, each of them with
double gunshot wounds through their heads.

Ma'tee's heart dropped when he saw his daughter
screaming in the middle of the massacre scene. He hurried over to her and scooped her in his arms.

Miamor had followed him up the stairs and was completely flabbergasted when she saw the slaughter. "Oh my
God," she whispered as she put her hand over her mouth.

Young Carter drove the van down the interstate while
Jay-Z's Reasonable Doubt pumped out of the factory
speakers. He looked in his rearview mirror and saw

Money and Mecca, both dressed in baggy clown suits and size forty-four shoes, taking off their wigs and wiping off the clown face paint.

"Damn!" Mecca yelled as he forcefully snatched off his red wig. He was totally enraged that he didn't get a chance to kill Ma'tee. "I didn't see him. He was on the pool patio, and then when I snuck back in, he was gone. I should have popped him when I first saw him, but he had a guard by the door."

"He must've ducked off somewhere to smash that female that came in," Money added, noticeably discouraged also.

Carter got off on the highway and pulled into an empty parking lot, where Mecca's Lamborghini was waiting. "We'll get 'em next time," he said confidently, throwing the "clown" van in park.

Mecca peeled off the costume and jumped into his car. "If there is a next time. Because of what we just did, Ma'tee's security is going to be extra tight. We may never get that close to him again. Fuck!"

Carter and Money jumped in with him, and they pulled off on their way back home. They had just sent a clear message—The Cartel wasn't about to lie down.

Chapter Six

"In the middle of a war, there's no room for weakness."
—Young Carter

Miamor sat Indian-style next to her sister's grave, her spirit broken and feeling weak without her big sister in her life to guide her. Anisa was the reason why Miamor had been put on to the street life. She had taught her everything that she knew, and now she was lost forever at the hands of the game. Miamor had always known that the possibility of death was high, because of the lifestyle that she and her crew led. The same way that she was willing to murk a mu'fucka with no ifs, ands, or buts about it, she knew that somebody, somewhere, was willing to do the same thing to them. She just never thought that it would happen to Anisa at the tender age of twenty-five. If she could turn back the hands of time, she would have definitely done things differently that night. It wasn't her idea to use Anisa as a pawn, but she was outvoted by the rest of the Murder Mamas, and the majority always ruled. Things are always so much clearer in hindsight, and she wished that she had convinced them to come up with a better plan to get at the notorious Cartel.

It had been weeks, and it was the first time she had been to visit Anisa's resting place. *This is all my fault,* she thought as tears formed in her eyes. She tried to fan her face to stop her tears from falling. She hated to cry, but it was no use. The tears trickled out of her eyes and stained her cheeks as she put her face in her hands, allowing her soul to release the pain.

"I'm sorry, Nisa. If I had been on point like I was supposed to be, this never would have happened," Miamor uttered out loud. She knew that wherever her sister was she could hear her.

She hadn't told anyone how she felt. Not even Aries and Robyn knew the guilt that she felt over her sister's untimely demise. She knew that the moment she lost sight of Mecca's black Lamborghini that her sister's life had been put on a countdown.

How did I let this happen? She felt the coldness from the grass that was still wet from the morning dew creep into her body. She shivered as she closed her eyes and thought of her sister's face. She bowed her head and prayed to God, feeling a closeness to Anisa that she'd never known while her sister was alive. *I'm sorry, Nis.*

Young Carter pulled his black Range Rover up to the cemetery and sat in his car for a moment to gather his thoughts. He was about to face his father for the first time. His first attempt had been interrupted by the Haitians, but now he had no excuse. It was time to make peace with the man who had created him. He got out of the car and walked up to the large monument that was his father's tombstone. He put his hand on it and leaned into the large marble, his head down. A spectrum of emotions shot through his body as he read the engraved inscription.

Carter Diamond Beloved Husband, Leader, and Father of Four "Diamonds are Forever"

He ran his hand over his face as he tried to contain the sorrow that took him over. He didn't know why he suddenly felt love for his father, but there was an unexpected connection between father and son that transcended even death.

"I know that you know that I'm here. I don't even know why I decided to stick around. For so long I wondered about you and why you left, why I never knew you. I understand now. I can't say that I can forget the abandonment that I experienced, growing up without a father, but I do forgive you. I swear on everything that I love that the mu'fuckas that are responsible for your death will never hurt the family." Carter began to walk away. He didn't think that there was anything left to say.

As he made his way back to his car, he stopped in his tracks when he saw the beautiful woman leaning against the passenger door. She was dressed in black Donna Karan slacks that hugged her hips and loosened at the leg, a black Donna Karan sweater, and silver Jimmy Choo stilettos. The closer he got to her, the more he recognized her face.

"Hi," she greeted as she stood with her silver clutch bag in hand.

"Damn, ma, I didn't peg you as the stalking type," he commented with a sexy smile.

A tiny dimple formed on the left side of his mouth, and that feature immediately became her favorite part of him.

"I was about to say the same thing, seeing as how I was here first," she replied, returning his smile with one of her own. "I saw you pull up just as I was leaving, so I decided to wait here for you. Who are you here for?"

"Just a family member, no one I was real close to," he responded. "I just wanted to pay my respects." He noticed that her eyes were red and swollen and there were bags underneath them. She looked tired and weak. Although she was still beautiful, there was something different about her. "You all right?" he asked.

"I'm"—She paused to think of the best way to describe her current state of mind—"surviving. My sister passed away a couple weeks ago. That's why I'm here." The woman shuffled nervously in her stance and looked at her feet.

"I'm sorry to hear about that."

"Yeah, me too." She stared off into space, and the tears returned to her eyes. She willed them away and shook her head as she looked back at Carter. "I'm Miamor," she said, offering her hand to him.

"Oh, I'm worthy of a name this time?"

Carter chuckled as he took her hand into his and shook it gently. Her name, exotic enough to complement her around-the-way features, fit her perfectly. Her brown shoulder-length layers were curled loosely and shaped her almond-colored skin. Her white teeth composed the perfect smile, and her M•A•C cosmetics were applied just right, not too much, but enough to make her skin glow.

"I told you, if you were worth my time, I'd see you again." She tiptoed and peeked at the tattoo that displayed his name. "Carter," she said aloud.

He noticed how she never let go of his hand as she intertwined her fingers with his own. The sound of his name rolling off her pouty lips was enticing, and he couldn't help but to be intrigued by her.

"It was nice to meet you," she stated as she walked away. She didn't let go of his hand, until she was forced to, because of the widening distance between them.

As he watched her strut away, she waved one last time and got into a silver Nissan Maxima and pulled away. Carter shook his head from side to side, grateful for her departure. He knew that if he ever got to know Miamor, she would be his weakness. He smiled to himself as he watched her car disappear around the corner and then hopped into his own vehicle and departed. *In the middle of a war, there's no room for weakness. Love will get you killed,* he thought as he made his way back to the Diamond mansion.

Breeze stood in the dining room over the kitchen table and argued as her mother, uncle, and twin brothers ate breakfast. "Uncle Polo, I'm not going out with this big, ugly bodyguard attached to my hip! How am I supposed to chill with my girls with him following me everywhere?"

Polo told her, "It's not negotiable, Breeze. You are not to leave this house alone. One of our men will escort you wherever you need to go. If you don't like that arrangement, you better ask one of your brothers to accompany you?"

"I got plans." Mecca stated quickly.

Breeze rolled her eyes at Mecca and hoped that her other brother would come to her rescue. "Money, please?" she begged.

"Sorry *B*, no can do. Uncle Polo and Young Carter set up a meeting between me and the board of advisors at Diamond Realty. I'm going to be taking that over, and I need to sit down with the board to make sure that they understand that this is still a family business—"

"Yeah, yeah, whatever."

"Who said you were going to be the one to take over the real estate company?" Mecca inquired.

"Young Carter and I discussed it," Money replied. "We think it's best."

"And I didn't have a say in this decision?" Mecca asked in irritation.

Young Carter overheard the conversation as he walked into the room. "No, you didn't, Mecca." He gave both Breeze and Taryn kisses on the cheek, and then patted Polo on the back. "There is enough responsibility for all of us to get in on some part of the business. The real estate company is where Monroe needs to be. We need to keep one of us clean and legal, now that we are at war with the Haitians. We never know where this might lead, and the less Monroe is involved, the better." Carter slapped hands with Monroe and then sat down at the table.

Polo smiled at Young Carter's authoritative approach when dealing with his younger brothers. He knew that it was only a matter of time before the young man assumed a leadership position in The Cartel.

"Yeah, you're right," Mecca responded hesitantly as he slapped hands with his older brother. Mecca still didn't like the fact that Carter had appeared out of the blue claiming to be his father's son, but the more he got to know Young Carter, the more he respected him. There wasn't a doubt in anyone's mind regarding his bloodline, and he was slowly beginning to warm up to the idea.

"Have you eaten, Carter?" Taryn asked.

"No, I haven't."

Taryn stood to fixed him a plate and put it in front of him.

"Thank you."

Breeze whined as if she were still a child. "Uncle Polo?"

Polo sighed and pointed his fork at Young Carter. "Will you tell your sister that she doesn't need to leave the house without one of the men?"

Carter asked, "Where you need to go, Breeze? I'll take you,"

"Thank you. At least one of my brothers is willing to do something for me," she stated in playful exasperation. She grabbed Carter by the hand. "Come on, let's go. We'll get something to eat later."

Carter grabbed one last forkful of eggs and put it in his mouth before Breeze pulled him out of the kitchen.

Taryn laughed out loud at the sight. "Looks like Breeze has found one more man to spoil her. That child is rotten," she stated with a smile on her face.

Carter maneuvered the Range Rover in and out of the Miami traffic as his sister sat in the passenger side, the huge Ralph Lauren sunglasses covering most of her face.

"I haven't gotten a chance to kick it with you much, with everything that's going on." Carter wanted to know how his presence in Miami affected Breeze.

"I know it seems like the only thing everyone has been worried about is The Cartel. It feels like I'm living out some old gangster movie or something. I just want things to be normal again," she replied, looking out of the window.

"So what's your take on everything that's happened?"

"You really wanna know?" Breeze pulled her glasses from her face and rested them on top of her head.

Carter nodded his head and waited for her to answer the question.

"I feel cheated because I only got to know my father for nineteen years. I loved him, and I wanted him to be there when I got married, and when I had my first child. I wanted him to be here for me. I feel like, now that he's gone, everything is going downhill. My mom is afraid every single day that the Haitians are going to harm us. Since meeting you, Mecca has become extra hard. It's almost like he's trying to prove himself to you. It's like he wants to make sure that everyone knows he is Carter Diamond's son. Monroe is the same, Uncle Po is the same—"

"And what about you?"

"Me, I'm dealing with everything the best way I know how. I cry every morning when I think of my Poppa. It's like one minute I'm upset with God for Him taking my father away, and then the next minute, I'm thanking Him for bringing you into our lives when He did. You are my brother, and I am glad that you're here, Carter. I don't know how, but you make things seem like they'll be okay."

"I'm just here to help, Breeze. At first, I wanted to say, 'Fuck Miami,' and move on with my life as if none of you ever existed, but that would be selfish. And I've never had a family, so I want to get to know you, Mecca, and Monroe."

"Well, I can tell you the way to win my heart," she said with a smile as bright as the summer Miami sun.

"How's that?"

"Everything today is on you."

"I got you, sis."

Breeze found out that she and Carter shared the same love for fashion. She took him from store to store as she shopped, picking up every designer she could find. He didn't complain or rush her in the same way her other brothers did, and he even gave honest opinions when she asked about an outfit she tried on.

"How's this?" she asked as she walked out of the dressing room in Saks Fifth with a skintight Seven jeans that fit low on her hips, almost revealing the crack of her ass, and a Fendi blouse that barely covered her breasts.

It was sexy, but definitely not something that he wanted his sister to wear. "I'm not buying that shit. As a matter of fact, you ain't wearing it even if you buy it yourself, so you might as well hang that back up." He flipped through his Apple iPhone, ignoring her.

"Come on, Carter, it's not that bad," she argued.

He didn't respond, and just continued to focus on his phone.

"You're just as strict as Poppa was," she stated with a little bit of attitude and a laugh. "I am a grown-ass woman, you know, big-head-ass."

"I heard that," he stated calmly as he leaned back in the leather chair, still flipping through his phone. He shook his head once she disappeared behind the dressing room curtain. As he waited for her to come out again, he mumbled to himself, "She gon' have me fucking these little niggas up in Miami."

They went through several outfits, and he had a comment for each one.

"Nah."

"That's whack, sis."

"That shit don't match."

Breeze went in and out of the dressing rooms until she finally grew tired of his disapproval. "Okay, Carter," she said, "out of all the stuff I've tried on, you've only liked three outfits. You tell me what's hot."

Carter put his phone on the clip of his belt buckle. "A'ight, let me show you how to do this. All that hooker shit you and your girlfriends be wearing is trash."

"Excuse me, everything in my closet cost a grip," she replied, one hand on her hip.

"That doesn't mean that it's classy. I'm a man, so I know what I'm talking about." He quickly located ten different items for Breeze to try on. "You want these niggas to respect you out here, especially you. You're the only daughter of Carter Diamond. You need to dress like the princess that you are and make men come at you correct when they checking for you."

"I hear you." Breeze took the items from his grasp. She tried on the first outfit, which was a pair of cropped white Ferragamo pants that hugged her shape as if it were tailor-made just for her body. Her white shirt had a sharp collar, dipped low in the cleavage area, and fit snugly around her slim waist, her sleeves stopping short just above her elbows, and a large black fashion belt adorned her waist. She slipped her feet into a pair of black stilettos. She had to admit, the outfit was nice and made her look like a kingpin's daughter.

She walked out of the dressing room and did a full spin for her brother.

"That's more you," he stated as he stood to his feet. He checked his presidential Rolex and noticed that they had been shopping for hours. He called one of the store associates over to them. "Can you have these items boxed and bagged for us?" he asked.

The woman grabbed the items from Breeze as she changed back into her clothes.

"Let's grab something to eat before we head back," he said as they walked out of the store.

"I know just the place. It's right up the street," Breeze responded as they walked out of the store. Breeze had at least five bags in each hand as they walked the distance to the restaurant.

Carter followed her across the street and into an elegant building that was made of marble and glass. He looked up at the sign that read *Breezes*. He looked at her in confusion.

She smiled. "Poppa bought it for me on my tenth birthday."

Carter nodded, and they entered the restaurant to have a late lunch. There was a long line of patrons waiting to be served. The establishment was crowded, so they inched through the crowd until they reached the hostess.

"Hello, Ms. Diamond," the hostess greeted, obviously recognizing Breeze. "Right this way."

There were groans and complaints from the people who stood waiting, but Breeze and Carter eased right past them and into the lavish environment. The voice of Billie Holiday filled the darkened space, and all eyes seemed to be on Breeze.

As they passed the bar, Carter saw Miamor sitting on a stool with two other women and he winked at her as he passed by. When they arrived at their table, Carter pulled out the chair for his sister and then sat across from her.

Aries' eyes followed Breeze and Carter to their table. "Miamor, isn't that de guy from de Casino?"

"Yeah, that's him." Miamor's arched eyebrows frowned at the sight of him. A twinge of jealousy crept through her heart, but she knew that she had no right to be upset. She didn't even know Carter. Just because she was feeling him a little didn't mean anything.

"Damn, is that his girl?" Robyn asked.

"Must be," Miamor replied, her tone a bit more sarcastic than she intended.

"Me know you ain't green?" Aries teased.

"Hell nah!" Miamor exclaimed. "Jealous for what? I don't even know the nigga. Yo, for real, it ain't even that serious. Since when have you ever known me to be that type?"

"Whoever chick is, she's rocking them Prada shoes." Robyn nodded her head in approval.

Miamor rolled her eyes and sipped at her drink as she tried not to focus on Carter.

"What are you looking at?" Breeze asked.

"Just a friend," he replied.

Breeze turned around and stared toward the bar at the three young women that had so much of her brother's attention.

"You making friends like that already? You've only been here a couple weeks."

"It's not like that, so get your head out of the gutter."

Breeze laughed again. It was refreshing to see her smile. It was then that Carter realized that he had never seen his sister's smile, and it looked good on her. This was the first time that he'd ever seen her happy.

She peeked back at the girls one more time and then whispered, "Which one is she?"

"The one in all black," he replied as he watched Breeze look back. "Quit staring, Breeze."

"Shit, she's staring back," Breeze shot back. "She must think I'm your girlfriend or something, because her face is all twisted up." Breeze giggled. After she took a sip of water from her water goblet, she said, "You better go talk to her because she looks mad."

Carter looked past his sister's head and saw the look on Miamor's face. He stood from the table and looked down at Breeze. "I'll be right back."

Robyn turned on her bar stool. "Don't look now, but here come your boy. I think I need to use the bathroom. Come on, Aries."

"What you mean, come on? Me don't have to go with you," Aries stated with a devilish grin. She licked her lips at the sight of the dark man walking toward them.

"Aries!" Miamor whispered.

"Why me have to go with she?"

"Because she doesn't want you all in her face, bitch. Now, come on." Robyn laughed and pulled Aries away.

Miamor laughed for the first time since her sister died, and Robyn winked at her as they disappeared around the corner.

Carter slid into the seat next to Miamor. "Why is it that you're everywhere I seem to be?"

"I don't know, but if I had known that you and your girlfriend would be here, I would have gone somewhere else," she replied with an attitude.

Carter smiled at her jealousy. They barely knew each other, yet she was already staking her claim.

"Don't be like that." He scooted his stool closer to her and whispered in her ear, "I'm only interested in one woman in this room."

She smiled, but scooted her own stool away from him. "I don't want to have to fuck your girlfriend up, so don't start no shit," she said seriously.

"That flip lip you got don't suit you, ma. I'm gon' have to grow you up."

"Oh, really. I can't wait to see you try to do that because a man can't change anything that I don't want him to. I'ma do me, regardless. I most definitely ain't changing for a nigga that already got a chick." Miamor turned to see Breeze walking toward them. "Here comes your girlfriend. You better make sure she acts right." Miamor faced the bar and sipped her strawberry daiquiri.

Carter shook his head as he watched his sister approach. He definitely wasn't impressed by Miamor's feistiness, but he liked a challenge. He knew that it wouldn't take long for her to fall in line, so he let her smart mouth slide for the moment.

"I just got a phone call from Mommy. I told her that we'd do take-out and bring dinner home," Breeze stated when she walked up.

"That's fine with me, but first I want to introduce you to a friend of mine. Breeze, this is Miamor. Miamor, this is my *sister*, Breeze," he said with a wicked smile.

Miamor, an embarrassed expression on her face, cut her eyes at Carter. He had let her sweat and show her jealousy, when all along he was with his sister. She smiled and shook the girl's hand. "Nice to meet you, Breeze."

"You too," Breeze replied.

Carter stood to leave and didn't say a word as he walked away from Miamor and headed for the door.

No, this nigga didn't. Miamor watched his back as he made his way through the crowd.

Carter stopped at the hostess' desk and wrote a note to Miamor. He asked the hostess, "Can you hand this to the young lady at the bar?" handed her a twenty-dollar tip, and then left out behind Breeze.

The hostess tapped Miamor's shoulder. "Excuse me, miss."

"Yes?"

"The gentleman that just left asked me to give you this." The hostess dropped the folded piece of paper on the bar.

"Thank you," she replied as she eagerly opened it.

Meet me at the end of the South Pier tonight at midnight. Don't front like you ain't coming, ma. Do

yourself a favor and be there. I want to get to know
you, Miamor.

    Carter

    PS: Dinner is on me

  Miamor smiled as her friends reappeared at the table.
"What did he say?" Robyn asked.

  "Nigga didn't say nothing," Miamor said. "He came
over here to tell me that chick is his sister, that's all."

  The friends resumed their conversation, and Miamor
threw in an occasional comment to make them think
that she was paying attention, but her mind was on
Carter. She was definitely going to the pier that night.
She checked her cell phone to see what time it was and
immediately started counting down the minutes until
she saw Carter again.